The Hero Within

Volume Two

Power

Yeral E. Ogando

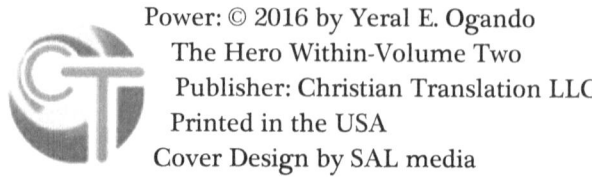

Power: © 2016 by Yeral E. Ogando
The Hero Within-Volume Two
Publisher: Christian Translation LLC
Printed in the USA
Cover Design by SAL media

Scripture quotations are from the King James Version of the Bible.

ISBN 13: 978-0-9966873-7-9
ISBN 10: 0-9966873-7-8

Library of Congress Cataloging-in-Publication Data
Ogando, Yeral E.

Title: /Power
ISBN 13: 978-0-9966873-7-9 (paperback)

1. Series Fiction 2. Spiritual Warfare 3. Christian .4. Inspirational
Title. Library of Congress Control Number: 2016916500

DEDICATION:

This book is dedicated to the Unique and forever-lasting person who has always been there for me, no matter how stubborn I am:

GOD

I also want to dedicate this work to you who have read *AWARENESS* and were waiting to read *POWER.* Thank you very much for your comments and ideas. Without you I would not have been here.

You all have a special place in my heart.

Always.

ACKNOWLEDGMENTS:

Thanks to God for giving me the strength to write the second volume of "The Hero Within" series.

Thanks to my editor, Sharon A. Lavy and SAL media "Cover Design" for doing such a great job helping me polish this book.

It has been an incredible journey after having completed *AWARENESS* and continuing the series with *POWER*.

Thanks to my father, Hector, my sister Estaunis and my daughters, Yeiris & Tiffany for staying by my side through this new experience. You know I love you.

Thanks to all of you for your continuous prayer and support throughout this second experience and especially to those of you who were eager to get your hands on *POWER* and quench that thirst left by *AWARENESS*.

For if a man think himself to be something, when he is nothing, he deceiveth himself. Galatians 6:3 (KJV)

Chapter 1

As he slouched back in his chair in the emergency room, Anthony Markson's eardrums felt ready to explode from the pain. The strange sound building in his ears almost drowned out things he desperately needed to hear. Like the questions the doctor and nurse had asked him.

The others reported they could remember nothing but the horror and darkness they had gone through in the locked room.

But Anthony remembered it all, and he was ashamed to have led his team into such a trap.

While some on the team were severely wounded, he had to admit, his worst injuries were to his pride.

Pride goes before destruction. How well he knew. But how painful was the lesson.

He needed to clear his head and help the other team members before fear overtook and claimed them all.

~*~

The ER buzzed with activity. Nurse Erin

Ludwig could barely keep up as she went from one cubical to another.

As if things weren't bad enough, that horney Tadd James had brought in Erin's best friend, Abby Power, along with three other injured people.

Not long ago, Erin had advised Abby to set her boundaries when Tadd began to come on too strong with his interest.

This evening he'd mentioned something about a dark room and vampire bats. *A likely story.* Erin would investigate the real reason that left her friend severely hurt with a broken arm and injures all over her once beautiful face.

"These teeth marks are huge," Erin said as she cleansed Abby's wounds with virus-killing liquid. "Could they really be from bats?"

If Tadd was to blame for Abby's wounds, he would definitely hear more from her.

Erin suspected Anthony would have some answers, and when she was finished here, she would question him further, along with the others who'd come in with them.

"This patient needs to be admitted," the doctor addressed Erin. "Get an injection of HRIG ready."

"Did anyone think to bring one of the creatures in with the victims? Either way, we better get the procedure started to check for rabies."

"Find out exactly where this old building is and notify the authorities to check it for bats. Depending on their findings we may have to treat the other patients in this group for rabies as a precaution."

~*~

In the next cubical, Dr. Sandra Beazel revealed a swollen ankle, and mentioned the bruises all over her body.

"Can you tell us what happened?" Erin asked.

"Five of us went to Slattersville to check out office space to rent. We didn't expect it to be so dark in the building, but without the electricity hooked up—" She sighed. "Anyway, I fell into a hole in the floor and as you can see I hurt my ankle."

"I'll send you to x-ray first and see what we need to do for your ankle," the ER doctor said.

Erin touched Sandra's forearm. "And Abby? Did she fall into a hole as well?"

~*~

Erin and the doctor moved to the next cubical to check out a man named Chris Parker.

He was bruised and battered and could hardly move. They suspected a head injury when nothing he said made any sense.

The doctor recommended pain medicine for Chris while they checked the other patients.

~*~

Tadd James had more cuts than Erin had first noticed when he'd arrived in the ER.

"Let me clean these wounds."

"How is Abby? Is she going to be all right?"

"You know I can't discuss the other patients with you." Erin tried to hold back her irritation with the man. After all, everyone who came to this hospital deserved the best care and courtesy.

~*~

After Sandra came back from x-ray Erin finished cleaning her injuries.

"You are one lucky lady," the ER doctor said. "Your ankle is fractured but all the bones are in place."

"So I get a cast? Can I choose a pretty color like the children often get now days?"

"I see you have a sense of humor. But with the swelling you have we are going to use a brace first. We will check on you weekly. When the swelling goes down we may apply a cast."

"So how long—"

"No weight bearing on the ankle for a minimum of six weeks."

"Crutches?"

"I was thinking if your insurance will go for it we have the hands free crutch with a pad to hold your leg bent at the knee and straps to your thigh. Or the knee scooter is an option, but it's a little more pricy, and won't leave your hands free."

~*~

By the time Erin checked on Chris again he was feeling better, but still seemed unable to understand what had happened.

The ER doctor took Erin aside and discussed the situation with her. "Since we don't know the man, perhaps he is simply one who is easily confused."

"You mean he may always be *a brick short of a load?*"

"Well, yes. To put it bluntly. On the other hand he may be in shock. But the symptoms don't really add up to it being entirely that either."

"So, will you admit him?"

The doctor approached Chris's bed. "Our rooms are pretty full. If you have someone at home to watch over you tonight I can write you up a prescription and send you home."

"I share a small apartment with Anthony Markson. Will he be released as well?"

"I'll let you know."

~*~

"How are they?" Anthony asked as the ER doctor approached him. "How is our team holding up?"

"We have the rest of your group patched up for now. Just to be on the safe side we better examine you as well."

Anthony held out his arms. "As you can see I don't have a scratch on me."

"Will you be able to watch over your housemate, Chris Parker?"

"Of course."

"Okay, here is what you have to do." The ER doctor held out a paper and went over the symptoms for Anthony to watch for. "Wake him up every hour."

When the paperwork was finished and Tadd and Chris were released, Anthony assured Erin they would be back to check on Abby in the morning.

Chapter 2

The next morning Anthony, Chris, Sandra and Tadd returned to the hospital and gathered in Abby's room.

Her nurse, Erin was taking her vitals. "Good morning. I'll be finished here soon. But you might as well know, Abby is my best friend so I am going to be very protective of her."

What's with this gal? Was the nurse blaming them for Abby's injuries? At her words Anthony felt dirty and covered in shame. "I can assure you she is a good friend to the rest of us as well."

"Hi, Anthony." Erin acknowledged him with a nod. "I remember meeting you at church. But I just met the others last night." She shot a questioning look at Tadd.

He held up his hands in mock defense. "I would have been at church with you guys last week but I had to work."

"And Chris Parker recently arrived from New York," Anthony said.

Erin laughed. "I gathered that, since he talks just like you and Janet."

"Speaking of Janet." Abby spoke with a very raspy and low voice. "Can you call and tell her where we are?"

Anthony slapped his hand to his forehead. He had completely forgotten about his sister with all the trauma of yesterday's disaster. What kind of brother was he? He'd checked Chris through the night as the ER doctor had insisted, but he hadn't even checked Janet's room that morning. *Lord, I can't do anything right. I am not worthy.*

"Janet came in two nights ago," Erin said. "She was in some kind of tornado and it affected her eyes."

"Are you talking about my sister?" Anthony stiffened to attention.

"That's right. Janet Markson."

"Where is her room?" Anthony asked. "I need to go see her."

"Let me bring her here, instead." Erin turned and headed toward the doorway. "Then all of you can see her."

"I'll go with you," he said.

"Ok, follow me." Erin motioned with her head. We'll be back in a few, Abby."

~*~

"Janet, what happened to you?" Anthony asked as he entered her room.

"Anthony, is that you?"

"Yes, sister. I just found out where you were. I'm sorry for not being here for you, earlier."

"You're here now," Janet said with a smile.

12

"That's what counts. I've been wondering about your trip."

"I have bad news about that. Abby was injured yesterday and the other team members are in her room across the hall. Would you like to go see her? Erin and I can take you over there."

"Abby's hurt? Yes, of course, I want to see her. I heard some commotion and wished I could roam the halls freely. But I have this little problem with my vision."

"Erin mentioned something about that," Anthony said. "Sounds like you had quite an ordeal. The rest of the team will want to hear more about it as well."

The three of them soon arrived at Abby's bedside. Anthony found a chair for Janet and stood beside her.

Sandra sat in the chair on the other side of Abby's bed, and the others leaned against the wall.

"I must apologize to all of you." Anthony looked at each one in the room. "I failed as your leader and have driven you into this situation where we find ourselves. My pride blinded me when I depended on myself instead of waiting to hear from God."

Each of the others watched him expectantly. Then he turned to Janet.

"I'm sorry I brushed off your questions about

whether I'd asked God specifically about going to Slattersville. Even when we see the hand of God at work we can't get ahead of His timing. And I'm afraid that is what happened here."

"Anthony, I'm also sorry I brushed off your concern for me in going to see Pastor Joe alone."

"Okay, but first, let's pray for repentance before sharing our views and experiences with one another," Anthony said.

As one, they bowed their heads and closed their eyes while Anthony led them in prayer.

"Lord, we have sinned against you. We come before you broken and wounded. Please forgive me because I was supposed to be the leader. Forgive me for letting my pride blind me to your will and your timing. Embrace me and tell me how to proceed from here. We all need you more than ever. We acknowledge our weakness. The enemy has hurt us, but we have learnt our lesson. We are down but not defeated. We truly want to serve only you. Holy Spirit, shine into our minds and hearts. Sweet Jesus let your grace be with us and in us all. Amen."

"Amen," the team responded.

Anthony smiled at his friends. "Welcome to this unofficial team meeting. For those of you who are not members of the team, we acknowledge that you have also suffered in our most recent battle. Continue to pray as you listen in on the meeting and then decide if you have been called to serve with us. We will certainly understand if our recent experience turns you away and I apologize again for my poor leadership."

"Fair enough," Chris said.

"Let's each share a little bit about ourselves. I'll begin by telling you I'm Anthony Markson, a lawyer by profession, and formerly from New York. I'm married to Becky and co-parent of our rowdy six-year-old son Ben. I had turned my back on God for a time, but He called me to lead this team and changed my name to *Warrior*."

Anthony squeezed Janet's hand so she would know she was next to speak.

"I'm Anthony's sister, Janet Markson. I have served the Lord for years, but He recently called me to join this team alongside of my brother. God has named me *Faith-woman*."

She smiled as another thought came to her. "Oh yes. I was a history teacher in New York, but I'm currently working at Clanston State Prison. Still single."

The others laughed and some of the tension left the room.

"Abby Power, sorry I can't speak very loud. I've been a Christian for many years. I was a nurse at this hospital, but I'm currently working at the clinic at the prison where Michael resides.

God recently named me *the Discerner.*"

"Tadd James, recent believer and interested in joining the team. No new name yet."

The others chuckled and the room seemed a little brighter.

"I was a prison guard at the state prison here in Clanston," Tadd continued. "But I have been transferred to the close security prison at Slattersville. The town where we were beat up."

"Chris Parker. I've been a Christian for many years and served in a children's ministry in New York. Then I heard about the work of this team, and I'll admit I came out of curiosity. And now I'm injured but not defeated. I am happy, because even though I don't understand it all, I know God has great plans for us."

"Dr. Sandra Beazel, but my friends call me Sandra. I have been a Christian for twenty years, and being a psychologist I have learned many things. I was intrigued by the work of this team from the moment Deborah told me about it, and here I am. I can't say I understand what has recently happened, any more than Chris does. I am willing to go the next mile if God calls me to walk with the rest of you."

"How refreshing that we can all say we are down but not defeated," Anthony said. "I'd like our newest friend to introduce herself as well."

"Thanks," said Erin. "I'm Erin Ludwig, I have

been a Christian for a long time, and I'm Abby's best pal as I already told you. I work here in the ER as a nurse. This is all so interesting. If you'd allow me, I would like to stay for the entire meeting."

"Of course you're welcome to stay," Anthony said with a nod.

The others nodded their agreement as well.

"This is not a full team meeting since we are missing two of our members. Our beloved brother, Michael Reeves, is in Clanston state prison at the moment. He's an ex-soldier. His wife Deborah, who Sandra mentioned, has also been a blessing to this team. They've allowed our first office to be located at their place."

"Oh, yes," Erin said. "I remember meeting Deborah at church."

"That's right." Anthony nodded. "And we are also missing Josh Pennington, who is a prisoner at Slattersville. Josh came to the Lord by the work of God through Michael in the prison in Clanston."

"And," Abby said. "Josh was also used by the Lord to save me from Big Jax."

"And we are thankful for that," Anthony said. "Now let's examine where we are as team, and share our experience from our most recent battle. Then, of course, we want Janet to share her story, since we still don't have much information about that tornado."

"Please let Janet speak first," Abby croaked.

"Okay, sis. Sounds like you have the floor."

"I know nothing about a tornado," Janet said as her eyes widened. "I was at Pastor Joe's house, and something happened to him. I can still picture the scene that greeted me when he opened the door. Glass and broken objects littered the floor in his living room. God prepared me for battle but a great darkness engulfed me and the next thing I knew I was waking up in the hospital."

"Maybe we can learn more about it from Pastor Joe."

"I hope so," Janet said. "When I woke up I could not see anything. I thought I was still at Pastor Joe's house and that someone had undressed me and put me to bed. It was pretty scary until Erin came into the room."

The whole room filled with a bright light, and an army was revealed. The heavenly warriors knelt in reverence to the Elite Commander.

"*My dear children*," God spoke in an audible voice.

"*I, the Elite Commander have chosen each of you in this room today for a greater purpose. Hear my voice and follow my instructions. You have been hurt because you deviated from my plans and tried to create your own. I have given specific gifts to each one of you, and they will be revealed in time. Right now you all need healing."*

A strong force washed across the room and Erin fell to her knees. Her body was instantly clad in full armor with her new name written on her right shoulder *The Mender.*

"Meet the new member of the team," the Elite Commander said. *"Erin I have given you a new name. You are the Mender because I have given you the gift of healing; use it wisely, starting with your fellow team members. I have also sent someone who will instruct all of you in my ways and about the gifts you've received. Watch for him. His name is The Emissary."*

When the room returned to normal the team looked at one another. Amazement and wonder shown from their eyes.

Anthony put his hand on Erin's shoulder. "Welcome to the team, Mender."

"Thank you," Erin said as she laid her hand on Abby's forehead.

"I felt power surge through me," Abby said in her normal voice. Her countenance beamed. "I feel great. I want to go home."

Erin moved from Abby's bedside to the chair where Janet sat and rested her hand on her.

"I can see! Hallelujah!" Janet grinned at each one in the room. I can see all of you!"

"I know you are healed, and you know you are healed," Erin said as she walked around the bed and laid her hand on Sandra. "But you need to present yourself to the doctor to be released."

She laid her hand on Chris and Anthony then moved to Tadd. "I owe you an apology."

Tadd's eyes widened. "Me?"

"Yes," Erin said as she laid her hands on him. "When you brought Abby into the ER I was so sure you were to blame for her injuries."

"I'm sure you realize by now, Erin, that we were involved in spiritual warfare," Anthony said. "And it is not over."

"I see that now. So what is next for the team?"

"We will wait for the Lord to send the Emissary. And in the meantime, I think we all need some quiet time with the Lord. The Elite Commander said everyone in this room is part of His chosen ones."

"Yes, I stand corrected." Erin turned back to Tadd. "Will you forgive me?"

"Yes, and please know that I would never intentionally hurt Abby."

"Well, now that we have that out of the way, Abby and Janet need to check with their doctor and get officially released." Anthony continued, "Sandra why don't you just check in at the ER before you leave here. Then let's all meet at Deborah's one week from today."

Chapter 3

Apollyon didn't appreciate his adversaries gaining ground and taking power from him. He lost no time in summoning all his generals and soldiers together to discuss his magnificent plan to strike down the Lord's team.

Wrapped in black leather with boots of steel the evil commander's piercing fiery eyes darted into every corner of Hell as he watched his warriors arrive. A champion, successor to the demon throne, Apollyon reigned in evil and evil reigned in him.

With pride in his golden tan, he elevated his powerful arms. The six-pairs of leathery wings secured to his lean muscular body spread over his head and down to his feet.

Teeth-perfect, a spectacular smile rested on his face. He had to appear confident beautiful beyond belief. He would win this war. His voice was pitch-perfect as he raised his voice to sing a song of praise of himself.

His eyes flashed approval as his demon subjects danced to the sound. Then with an evil grin he finished his song.

~*~

Without warning, Apollyon unleashed his wrath. "Those bastards escaped from me, but I will bring 'em down," he screamed.

Everything and everyone in Hell trembled.

Botis stood before Apollyon and bowed low. "Malphas, Mastema, Samael, and Legion have arrived, My Prince."

For this gathering of Apollyon's warriors Botis presented as a gargantuan dragon. In this form he became a roaring, fire-breathing taste of imminent destruction. His impenetrable greenish-brown scales protected his core while his massive legs, feet, and tail were prepared to crush anything that stood in his way.

With one command from Apollyon, Botis would use his sharp claws of steel to slash the throat or tear out the heart of a victim as they dangled in his powerful grip.

Botis could also transform into the likeness of a human, and in this form he carried a gleaming silver sword laden with sharp projectiles from hilt to tip. But when he'd appeared in human form in the past his two horns and his large teeth spoiled his disguise.

"Wonderful," Apollyon replied. "Who is yet missing?"

"My Prince Amaros, Perdix, Succumbus, Eligos, and Asmodee have not yet arrived."

At this news Apollyon's rage increased by

thousands. "Where are they? They will pay for their insolence."

A few minutes later the remaining commanders from the evil forces arrived. "They are all here My Prince," Botis announced.

"You!" Apollyon immediately jumped the closest late arrival, knocking him on his back. Then he stepped on Amaros' throat. "I gave you a very simple mission to control Anthony's sister and you failed me."

"But My Prince." Amaros' voice came out in a squeak. "We have all failed."

Fire burned in Apollyon's eyes. "Botis," he called with a snap of his fingers.

Botis fired his dragon flame over all of the warriors gathered in the room.

The demon warriors backed away. "My Prince, please forgive us. We will bring them down," they screamed out their pleas in unison.

"Listen carefully then." Apollyon's voice became low and deadly. "We must find their weak spots and become part of their lives."

"Yes, My Prince." The demons groveled at his feet.

"Rise up. Do not disappoint me. I charge you to confuse, deceive, and destroy. Go."

~*~

Meanwhile, at Clanston state prison Michael and Big Jax studied the scriptures daily and grew in grace and holiness.

One night Big Jax had a dream. He found himself in the middle of all his friends from before he became a believer. Those who had been in his gangs eyed him with hatred, and grabbed him by force.

They tied him to a tree and were ready to chop off his head, when he heard a voice saying *"You are my son now, nothing will harm you."*

Suddenly Big Jax found himself at another place with another inmate who became his best friend.

He woke up with a pounding heart. Big Jax bumped the cot above his head. "Michael, you awake?"

"I am now. What happened, Big Jax?"

"I had another dream."

"Please tell me about it."

Big Jax told him the dream in full detail.

"My friend, the interpretation of your dream has been revealed to me. Although your former friends are looking to hang you and chop off your head, the Lord has other plans."

"Whew," Big Jax said. "That's good to know."

"A few weeks from now you will be moved to a different prison where you will meet another inmate. God has a mission for the two of you. He is one of my dearest friends and I know you will learn to love him as I do."

"A few weeks? What if they accomplish their plans before I get shipped out?"

"God told you nothing will harm you. He is in control."

"Sounds good to me." With a smile on his face, the giant of a man lay back down with sweet acceptance and soon went back to sleep.

~*~

The Emissary was uneasy. He'd promised to deliver the message from the Lord, and he knew he needed to tell the story to this group.

"I haven't been out of this town for years. Lord, please help me."

"Do not worry. I will bring them to you. But now it is time for you to go to the prison and visit my servant Josh," the Elite Commander spoke to the Emissary's heart.

~*~

A prison guard stood outside his cell. "Josh Pennington, you have a visitor."

His heart leapt within his chest. *The team has come.*

But when Josh got to the visitor's room he found an aged man with long hair sitting across the glass from him. The man's physique indicated he was or had been a soldier.

Josh picked up the phone. He had never seen this man in his life. Why was he here? "You have mistaken me for someone else, sir. But since you are here, how can I help you?"

"I am Daniel Samuels and the Lord sent me to talk to you." the muscular, but aged, man said.

"Are you telling me our Lord God the Creator sent you?"

"Yes, Josh."

"You know my name."

The man stood on his feet and Josh saw this warrior in full body armor with the name on his right shoulder of *The Emissary*.

"And you are part of God's army," Josh said. "But what does your name mean?"

"We are all given new names by God, if you still haven't gotten yours, do not worry. He will give you one in time," the Emissary said.

"We all have battles to fight and you have been chosen to join this team. You are the first one of the team I have met."

"The Lord used Michael Reeves, my good friend in Clanston state prison to rescue me from the darkness," Josh said. "I still miss him."

"My son, you need to be strong. Dark times are coming. You are needed to fight a big battle for the Lord."

"I am willing, and I sense you have a message for me."

"That's right. Although you will be released within a few weeks, you still have something to do here, first. Get ready, because your new partner will bring your biggest trial."

"What do you mean?"

"All I can tell you is that an old acquaintance is coming. He will need your help while you are both in here."

"Can you tell me anything else?"

"Just know that I will be waiting for you once you get out. I will be your guide and trainer for this new quest." Daniel Samuels put down the phone and left the visitors area.

Josh felt encouraged by the visit, and yet a bit anxious about the news Samuels had brought. But he was committed.

Lord, I am here, whatever you command me to do, I will surely do it.

Chapter 4

Being troubled in spirit the past few days, Becky had asked the members of New Beginnings church to pray for her husband and for Janet. So when the phone rang that evening she raced to pick it up after the first ring, expecting to hear Pastor Good's voice on the other end.

"Hey, Babe."

"Anthony! I am glad you called. I have been worried about you. Are you ok?"

"Yes, Honey, we are all fine. But I sure miss you."

"Ben and I miss you too."

"Have you thought any more about moving to Ohio?"

Becky was silent for a moment. Would she ever be ready for this? "I don't know Anthony. I'd need to get a job there and—"

"Do not worry about all that Becky, God will guide you in your decision."

When Becky heard this, instead of being reassured, her heart pounded.

"I am thinking of opening a law office here. You know it has always been my dream to go out on my own. I took the state boards about four weeks ago.

She gasped. He hadn't mentioned taking the test. But that meant he was setting down roots in Ohio for sure. "When will you know the results?"

"In two more weeks. But, Becky, I need you here."

"I know," she said with a sigh.

"Dad," Ben screamed.

"Wait. Let me put Ben on the phone."

"What's up, Slugger? How are you?"

"I'm great, and I've got you covered, Dad. I have been praying for you. Mom and I have both been praying. Has God been talking to you? Have you fought good fights? I want to see your armor. Dad? Dad? Are you there?"

"Slow down, Buddy," Anthony said with a chuckle. "You ask so many questions. I can't get a word in edgewise."

"Sorry."

"That's okay. Everything is great here too. I will see you in a few. I will be coming home for the weekend."

"Whoopee."

"Love you, Buddy."

"Love you, Dad. Bye."

"He's pretty wound up as you can tell," Becky said when she got back on the phone.

"I told him I plan to come home this weekend. I hope we can have a good discussion about our future. I miss you."

"We miss you too, Anthony. I love you and I'm eager to see you on the weekend."

The moment Becky hung up the phone, the Lord spoke to her heart. *It is time for you to support my servant Anthony. It is time for you to move to Ohio with your husband. He needs you by his side more than ever.*

She hung her head. "Yes, Lord. I am yours. I want to do your will. Please help me."

~*~

Michael started thinking about the departure of Big Jax. The beloved giant of a man had been such a blessing in filling the void that Josh had left when he was moved to Slattersville. Michael was already starting to feel lonely again.

"Michael, you are not going to be left alone. Your task here has been accomplished," The Elite Commander spoke to his heart.

"But, Lord, what does it mean? Am I going home?"

There was no answer this time.

A guard approached his cell. "You have a visitor, let's go."

Elation surged through Michael's body. Could it be Deborah, Anthony, or someone from the team?

When he reached the visitor room he saw his lawyer.

"Your behavior has been outstanding and you've had many recommendations. I have pulled some strings here and there. You are getting out of here in a week or two."

"Wow."

"Of course, you will still be in domiciliary arrest until you serve your time, but at least you will be at home."

"Thank the Lord," Michael said. "Thank you. Thank you. Thank you.

Michael almost floated back to his cell, he was so happy.

"Well, Decipher," he said to Big Jax. "You will be moving to a close security prison, and I am moving out of here to my home. Isn't it awesome?"

"Yes, indeed." Big Jax leaned over and put his hand on Michael's shoulder. "Do not forget to visit me in Slattersville."

"Of course, I won't forget."

~*~

New Hope Trinity Church was in mourning.

Pastor Joe had made it to the hospital on time, and seemed to be recovering. But the next day he had a heart attack and died.

The church members were devastated. And of course, Robert was sad and regretful.

"I was not there for you, Papa, please forgive me. But then, how could have God allowed such a thing, to take you away from me. You were the only one I had left."

As he talked, Robert's heart filled with anger, rage and vengeance. "Why Lord? Why did this have to happen to me? Why? Why?"

~*~

The service on Sunday night was beautiful as always, but something was missing. Everyone missed the presence of the late pastor Joe.

Reverend Robert's sermon was "*For to me, to live is Christ, and to die is gain. Philippians 1:21*". However he himself was not so convinced. Even while preaching he thought only about himself. *What about me? What is my gain? I only feel pain and sorrow.*

The church members offered their condolences and at the same time inquired about Janet and her health. They told the reverend how they planned to visit her at the hospital, having no idea she was no longer there.

~*~

The next morning, Janet's phone rang. She glanced at the caller ID and answered. "Robert, it's nice to hear from you."

"Hi, Janet, my apologies, I have not visited you because we have been busy with the funeral and mourning our loss."

"I'm sorry, Robert. I must have missed something. What funeral?"

A deep silence echoed across the line.

"My father's funeral," he finally said. "He had a heart attack the day after we took both of you to the hospital."

Janet could not speak, her heart pounded with pain and sorrow. The phone slipped out of her hand and dropped to the floor. A waterfall of tears spilled down her cheeks. "Oh, Lord. No, no, no." she wailed. "I can't bear it."

Anthony saw Janet fall and ran to her. "Janet. Are you ok? What is happening?

"He is dead."

"Who? Who died?"

"Pastor Joe. Oh Lord, no." Something in Janet's heart told her Joe's death was not natural. It had something to do with the spiritual battle at his home. Her tears stopped. She was determined to find out what was happening.

Anthony called the other team members and gave them the bad news. "Janet and I are heading to New Hope Trinity Church. I am sure Abby is already there. Let's all go and support the church."

"The others will be there," Anthony told Janet, Chris and Deborah as they prepared to leave.

So the four of them piled into Anthony's Porsche and they soon found themselves at New Hope Trinity Church.

All the church members had rallied around

Reverend Milton and paid their sympathy to him. They prayed for the loss to the church. The Team members offered words of comfort also.

When the moment was over, Abby gathered the team to one side. "I fear pastor Joe's death has something to do with our battles. There is something strange going on here in the church. We need to inquire of the Lord about it. We must pray and find the demon that wrecked Pastor Joe's house and injured him and Janet."

Janet nodded in agreement. "I feel that way too."

"We will all keep a close eye on this church and the new pastor, Reverend Robert Milton," Anthony said.

Chapter 5

After spending the week in constant prayer, the team felt the Lord's blessing to take a break for a week or two. It was time to organize their thoughts and get closer to their families. While they could not neglect prayer and staying close to the Lord, they did need to straighten up other lose ends in their lives.

On Thursday Anthony drove home and enjoyed time with his wife and son on Friday and Saturday.

Sunday they worshiped at New Beginnings Church. When they returned home after a delightful meal at Red Lobster, Ben went to the back yard and played with his cat.

"Becky, we need to talk. Please sit down in the living room with me," Anthony said.

"Alright."

Anthony took her hand. "I know things are kind of different and difficult to understand for you."

"Kind of." She looked up at him. "You are never around, so it's like I have no husband. Ben whines that he misses you all the time."

"I know Becky, but—"

"Anthony," Becky interrupted. "There is something I have not told you. It is not easy for me, but I guess it is time for you to know."

Anthony's chest tightened. *What is she talking about Lord? Not more problems, please. I don't know how much more I can take.*

"The Lord has spoken to me."

Relief washed over Anthony. "Thank you for telling me. It is so cool that you are building a relationship with Him."

"Please do not interrupt me until I finish."

"Ok, Honey. My lips are sealed." *Lord, help me to accept whatever comes.*

"I know I have not been supportive with your new call, but even if I do not agree or understand whatever you are doing, God has shown me I need to support you and be by your side."

Anthony's heart raced with joy. "Are you saying what I think you're saying?"

"This is so hard for me. Please do not interrupt."

"Sorry, Honey."

"I do not like your life to be in continuous danger, but I also understand that you have been changed. *The Lord has instructed me to move to Ohio and be with you.*"

Anthony jumped right out of his chair, raised his arms toward the ceiling and yelled. "Praise the Lord, halleluiah. Thank you, Lord." He stopped and glanced at his wife. "I'm sorry, Honey. Were you finished?"

Becky laughed and rose from her chair as well. She put her arms around him. "Amen."

"Allow me to go back to Ohio and organize everything. While I'm setting up my new office, I'll see if Abby has found something for you there. I've already asked her to check for some job opportunitys."

"How did you know I was going to say yes?" Becky asked.

"Well, I trusted in God and even when I had many doubts, I always had the hope you'd understand."

"Okay, Mr. Markson. You have your answer. Now. I need to inform the people at my work and at church. I need to tell my friends. It's time for Ben's school to start. Ack. So many things. My head is spinning."

"No worries, you start working on all these things you mentioned, and I will head back to Ohio and set up everything we will need."

The back door slammed as Ben entered.

"Hey, Buddy?"

"What, Dad?"

"You and Mom will soon move to Ohio with me. Before long we'll be together again."

"Awesome, Dad. Awesome. Will I see you in

your armor and watch you fighting enemies?"

"Well, I don't know. We'll see about that, Buddy. That's God's department, you know."

"Yes, Dad. And Mom won't cry anymore because you aren't here."

Becky laughed.

"Okay, Buddy. Let's go outside and toss some balls"

"Yay!"

~*~

Dr. Sandra Beazel increased her scripture reading and prayer times. But she found she had more and more questions for God. And over and over she heard that soft, gentle, and at the same time, strong voice stating that she was selected to be part of the team and fight battles against demons.

Then a few days later during her prayer time, she finally got some answers.

"*You are no longer called Sandra,*" the Elite Commander said. "*I have changed your name to Psychic. I have given you the gifts of Wisdom, Discernment and Prophecy. Get ready because fierce battles await you. You will be instructed on what to do by my servant.*"

"Yes, Lord." She bowed her head. *Where is that Emissary? Why does he not show up?*

Dr. Beazel had several consultations that day, but something had changed. She was aware of a difference in how she perceived the things her patients said and did.

AS soon as her next patient entered the office, she immediately felt the darkness on Mrs. Robinson. She'd been her patient for over six months now. Mrs. Robinson had many issues with her husband, but everything had seemed to be going better. And until that moment Dr. Beazel had not seen the real cause of her problems.

"Please have a seat, Mrs. Robinson."

Out of the darkness, a creature appeared behind Mrs. Robinson. The creature appeared as a beautiful woman wrapped in chains. She had long red hair and her thin body was covered with black stripes. The darkness soon encircled the creature with a big tag reading "Slave."

Psychic immediately understood the demon of slavery had been tormenting Mrs. Robinson for months.

With the discernment, Psychic was clothed in her battle suit, her armor covering her, and her new name appearing on the right shoulder.

"Time for battle," the Elite Commander said to her heart. "Do not fear I am with you."

"Dr. Beazel," Mrs. Robinson said. "I feel so depressed today. I feel like I just cannot continue anymore."

"I am here to help you. Just relax for a few

moments, and you will feel better shortly."

"You really think so, Dr. Beazel?"

"Yes, I am sure."

Mrs. Robinson appeared to fall asleep.

The demon suddenly transformed the tips of her chains into sharp and shiny blades radiating a black aura. The chains were now like razors. She grew a second head and both took on the triangular shape of a python, with fiery eyes.

Psychic stood up from her chair and got ready to fight when the two headed python threw hundreds of chain blades toward her.

Psychic used her gold shield to stop the blades and her shining sword to break them. The razor-sharp blades shattered and fell to the floor.

Swinging her sword, Psychic went for the head, but the two head python dodged her blade.

"She's mine," the demon claimed.

"*Do not fear*" *said the Elite Commander. Speak up to her using her name*" The Elite Commander spoke again to her heart."

Psychic shook her head. "Abdiel, I know who you are. Make no mistake, you will be defeated today."

"By you and who else, *Psychic?*" Abdiel laughed out loud. "I know who you are too. And I know you are much too weak to defeat me."

"Yes, you are correct, but I am not alone." As Psychic saw the spiritual army by her side, she gained strength and swung her sword with a cry, "I defeat you in Jesus' name." While the first snake head rolled down the floor, Psychic didn't notice the second one stab her in the back. But she felt the poison running through her veins.

With another blow, Psychic cut off the remaining python head. But even as it rolled across the floor, Abdiel managed to say, "That is not all. It isn't over yet." and then she vanished from the room.

Moments later Mrs. Robinson awoke. "Thank you very much for the session today Dr. Beazel. I don't know what you did, but I feel new relief. You are an angel," she said. "I feel like I am free at last."

"Have you ever tried visiting the church?"

Mrs. Robinson frowned. "What do you mean?"

"I think it is time for you to seek God."

"Oh. Find God in church. Yes, Doc, you are right. My mother took me to church when I was a young girl. I will follow your advice."

A knock sounded at the door. Erin Ludwig had just showed up at Dr. Sandra's office without calling or announcing her intentions.

"Sandra, are you ok?" Erin asked. "The Lord told me to hurry to you. He said you were in great danger.

Psychic was pale, and her veins were turning black. "I—I am fine," she said before she fell.

"Time to use your healing powers," said the Elite Commander.

The Mender took a closer look at Psychic's back and saw her ripped blouse and smelled the awful cut. She put her right hand over the wound, and Psychic's veins and skin returned to her natural color.

Sandra sat up. "Thank you Erin, you've saved me." The cut had completely healed over, and Psychic was breathing normally once again.

"No, The Lord saved you. I just heard His voice and came to His call. But, what happened here?"

Sandra shared the full story with Erin about how the Lord had changed her name and given her new powers. She told Erin about the fierce battle. "But we must talk to the team," she said. "I feel there is something more to it. That demon said '*It isn't over yet*' before she vanished."

Chapter 6

A prison guard held his baton against the bars of the cells as he and his partner marched down the row.

The day arrived for Michel and his cellmate to move from Clanston State Prison and go their separate ways.

Michael gave Big Jax a man hug. "I'm going to miss you, Buddy." The bittersweet feelings almost overpowered him.

"I'll miss you too. Even though some new guy is supposed to become my best friend, he'll never measure up to you. Remember to come see me in Slattersville."

"If the Lord wills, I will come. I'll be on some sort of probation for the next couple of months so I'm not sure how far I will be able to travel."

Michael watched Big Jax walk out of the cell and down the hall until he could no longer see any part of his jumpsuit.

He would miss the big guy, that was for sure, but it was time to return to the team. He hoped his early return would be a surprise for everybody. He grinned as plans danced in his head.

Now that he could focus his mind on home he realized the separation had made his heart long for his precious wife.

Why had he taken his frustration out on Deborah? Why had he been so angry and rude when she'd visited him? He realized he'd upset her greatly when she had never come back to see him at the prison.

"I need to apologize and show her how much I love her." Did she even want him to come home?

~*~

At Slattersville closed security prison Josh received the news through the prisoner's grapevine that his new cellmate Big Jax, *the dragon,* was coming to town.

He lowered his face to his hands. *Peace is over.*

Life in Slattersville prison had never been a picnic, but now this? Josh was terrified just hearing the name of this brutal and psychotic criminal.

And to make matters worst, they were bringing Big Jax to be his cell mate.

Of course Viper had been telling him that for days. Viper talked tough but he didn't scare Josh like Big Jax did.

"Lord, please. Help me."

"Let not your heart be troubled, neither let it be afraid," the Lord spoke to his heart.

Screams filled the air. "Big Jax is in town." One by one the prisoners in each cell took up the chant until the noise was deafening.

Viper Chambers, *the king snake,* just smiled. "Yeah, the boss is here, and just in time."

Fear clutched Josh's heart. "Why did you call him boss?"

"Cause he is the boss," said Viper in a raspy voice. "He ain't no game, he's the man."

Josh paced the cell. Back and forth. Back and forth.

"See ya, little rat," said Viper when the guard came to transfer him to another cell. "And let's see how much you want to talk with Big Jax."

He gave an evil laugh. "Remember how I told ya the snake swallows up the rats? Imagine what a dragon will do to a rodent like you."

~*~

The team members were amazed by the marvelous work of God. Michael was coming home after serving less than four months in prison.

With the news of his approaching arrival the others gathered to welcome this first and oldest member back to the team.

Everyone was eager to see him, talk to him and share the developments that had happened while Michael was gone. They wanted to share what they knew about God's unfolding plans.

Anxious and excited at the same time, Deborah wondered if the time in jail had changed Michael back to the ogre he had been before he became a Christian. Was he locked into the rage and abuse of the past?

At that moment, Abby Power, *the Discerner*, approached her. "Don't worry. Michael has not fallen back into the type of man he was. Ease your mind and heart, my dear friend. Your husband is truly a new man in Christ."

Deborah gasped. "How do you know what I'm thinking?"

"I'm sorry. Did I spook you a bit? God gave me the gift of discernment and asked me to comfort you."

Deborah laughed. "With this team and all the battles and power surging around here, anything is possible."

"Yes, Deborah, all things are possible with God."

~*~

Home sweet home. Michael was so revved up, he felt like a boy again.

His heart swelled as he opened the door to his house, eager to see his beautiful wife. "Oh how I missed my home. Thank you God for bringing me back."

He saw Deborah and ran toward her. "Hello, darling, I missed you so much." He hugged and kissed her until tears ran down her face. With a final kiss he let her go. "Thank you for waiting for me. Forgive me for being such a jerk."

"Surprise and welcome home!" the team yelled.

"Whoa." He hadn't even seen the others. "I wanted to be the one to surprise you guys. And you're all here. Hey, I even see new faces. We have a lot of catching up to do."

"We have plenty of time," Anthony said. "Perhaps you should have some rest now."

"Rest! What are you talking about, Brother Anthony? I have been resting long enough. A four month rest."

Everyone in the room laughed. It was good to be back and surrounded by his friends.

"All right." Anthony gestured toward the others in the room. "In that case, let me introduce you to everyone."

Deborah had slipped into the kitchen and came with snacks and juice.

Michael latched onto her again. "Oh, darling, I missed you so much."

"Me too, Mr. Reeves." She batted her eyes, patted him on his shoulder and left again.

Michael stared after her with mixed feelings. She seemed friendly enough, but eager to get away.

"Listen up everybody." Anthony raised his

hand for attention. "For those of you who have not met him yet, this is Mr. Michael Reeves the owner of the house. So even from prison he has been our host."

"Please," Michael said with a smile. "None of this mister stuff around here. I'm just Michael or brother."

"Michael was the first member of the team to join me. He and his wife, Deborah, have been a blessing to all of us."

He turned to Michael. "I'm sure you remember Janet, and Abby. Your two companions at the prison."

"Oh, yeah! I appreciated them a lot." He grinned at the women. "We have many war stories to share."

Abby bounced up and down like a child. "La, la, la, la, la. I got my job back at the hospital."

"So you are out of jail too?" Michael teased. "Glad you can share my home coming party."

She grinned and smacked him on the shoulder.

"Tadd James." With a gesture, Anthony continued the introductions.

"Hey, Tadd, what a pleasant surprise. I didn't know you were on the team."

"Yeah, many things have changed since I saw you last, Michael. I'm glad to see you on this side of the bars."

Michael laughed. "Me to, Brother. Me too."

"Erin Ludwig, a nurse at the hospital where Abby works."

"Awesome." Michael reached out and clasped her hand in both of his.

"And last but not least we have two more new members. Chris Parker from New York and Dr. Sandra Beazel."

"I see the Lord has been at work. Nice to meet all of you." Michael stretched his neck and searched the room to see where Deborah had fled.

"We're just missing Josh who is now in Slattersville," Anthony continued

"Man. I miss Josh. I wonder if my parole stipulations will allow me to visit him," Michael said.

"We will have to check on that," Anthony agreed. "But, anyway, now you know all the current members of the team."

"You are mistaken about one thing, Brother Anthony. We are missing two members."

"Who else am I missing?"

So Michael told the story about Big Jax, the battles they had fought, and how the Lord had called him. "And now he is going to Slattersville to be Josh's cellmate."

"But—" Abby's eyes were opened wide in surprise. "The dragon is the reason they sent

Josh to Slattersville."

"Yeah. That is what we thought at the time. However our friend is no longer Big Jax, *the dragon.* In fact, he is now, Big Jax. *The Decipher.*"

Tadd shook his head in wonder. "You have got to be kidding."

"That is incredible." Janet did a fist pump. "How great is our God."

"The Lord is amazing," Michael agreed. "We must visit Slattersville prison soon, because Josh has no idea about Big Jax's conversion."

"Yes, we've been meaning to visit him," Anthony said.

Michael held up his hand. "But wait. There is more. My brothers and sisters, my new name is *The Shrewder.*"

Abby clapped her hands. "Praise the Lord."

"Welcome home, Shrewder." Deborah said, as she came up behind him and wrapped her arms around his waist. "What does your new name mean?"

Abby grinned. "God has blessed your husband with the gift of wisdom."

The team laughed together with joy.

Then Anthony briefed Michael on the past events, the beating they'd received at the abandoned building in Slattersville, Erin's calling as healer, and how they were waiting for *the Emissary.*

"*It is time to go back to Slattersville, but do not fear, for I will be with you. You are to visit my two servants Josh and Big Jax.*" the Elite Commander spoke in an audible voice to the team.

They had a final prayer before they dismissed for the evening and the team agreed to continue visiting New Hope Trinity Church.

Chapter 7

It was late afternoon when Josh heard a rattle of chains against the bars.

"Open the gate," said one of the guards standing outside of his cell.

Oh, crap. Josh stared at the large prisoner between the two guards. *I am a dead man.*

The other guard twisted the key in the lock and the gate swung open. Then both guards pushed the prisoner inside and the first one grinned at Josh. "Say welcome to Big Jax. He's your new cellmate."

Josh could hear his knees knocking together as he backed away. But Big Jax did not raise his face, nor did he speak. He simply crawled onto the lower bunk and threw himself onto the mattress.

Didn't he see me? Did God make me invisible to him?

Josh leaned against the wall for support, afraid the big man would pounce on him any moment.

Darkness fell.

Big Jax continued sleeping.

Josh finally relaxed enough to climb into the

top bunk and stretch out. He didn't expect to sleep a wink, but sometime in the night he awakened and felt a hand over his mouth.

Oh, Lord, this time he is going to kill me for sure.

He almost screamed but Big Jax signaled him to be silent.

Dude, don't be afraid, I'm not going to hurt you," Big Jax whispered. "Don't scream when I remove my hand. Got it?"

Josh did his best to calm the shaking and nod.

Big Jax removed his hand.

"You called me Dude?"

"That is correct. But keep your voice down," Big Jax whispered.

"Do you even remember me?"

Big Jax laid his hand on Josh's shoulder. "Believe it or not, I remember you perfectly."

"And you don't want to kill me?" Josh knew he was blubbering.

"Chill out, man. Take it easy. I ain't going to hurt you. I just need to talk to you."

Josh finally remembered God's word "*Let not your heart be troubled, neither let it be afraid*" and he relaxed. "I'm listening."

"I'm sorry for whatever happened in the past," Big Jax said. "Something else was controlling me and commanded me to kill you."

Josh was speechless as he lay on his bunk and

listened.

"I am not that person anymore. When you left Clanston I was transferred to the cell with your friend Michael Reeves. My life changed after that."

"Wait a minute. If you were with my friend Michael, that means—?"

"Yes, Josh. I have been saved. By the way, Michael sent his regards."

"Man, I was shitting my pants when I heard you were coming here. I couldn't even sleep. I was so intimidated and frightened by you. I am still kinda shook. You really are a Christian now?"

"Shh. Yes, Josh, in fact, I am no longer the dragon, I am now *The Decipher.*"

"What on earth, man? You telling me God gave you a new name already?"

"Yes, He has."

"That is awesome, Brother, I cannot believe it." Josh's chin wobbled. "I haven't received a new name yet."

"Don't fret about it. I am sure it will come when the time is right," Big Jax said.

"But we have major problems now, and I need your help," he continued. "My old crew, my gangs are all here. They were waiting for me, expecting great things, you know. But I have changed, and I'm not who they think I am. Not anymore."

Big Jax ran his hands over his head. "Viper was my second in command. I don't know if you have met him, but he's—"

"Yeah, he was my cellmate before you came."

"What? And you are still alive? Wow. God has big plans for you, because Viper does not wait. He doesn't talk things over. He just goes for the kill."

The two new friends talked all night long, as Big Jax shared his dream with Josh.

"We need to pray for direction," Josh said. "Because like our friend Michael says, 'this is some heavy stuff.'"

~*~

At the evil one's den in Slattersville, Botis brought news that the team of bastards was going to pass over his master's town once again.

"The time has come," Apollyon said. "I will crush these parasites and bring them to ashes. These insects are nothing. They will not escape this time."

"Yes, My Prince." Botis lifted his head and flashed fire in a triumphant gesture.

"Call all our forces, generals, commanders. Get Malphas, Legion, Eligos, Mastema, Samaels, Abdiel, Asmodee, everybody. We need to gather for war." Apollyon gave an evil grin. "But this is not going to be a simple battle. Mark my words.

We are going to massacre them."

"Of course, My Prince." Botis stepped back and gave a bow.

"I want everyone here within twenty-four hours, because in two days these little rats will be here. I have the perfect trap for them. They won't know what hit them."

"It shall be as you wish." Botis turned and left to send out the message to the troops.

Before long, the cunning trap was set in position. The evil forces were ready to crash, kill, and destroy.

Chapter 8

Before they left on their trip to Slattersville, the following day, the team asked for God's guidance. When their eyes were opened to see the heavenly army accompanying them, the prayers lost their mournful pleading tone and took on a more optimistic note.

Although they were concerned about what they would find, this time they knew with certainty the Lord had sent them.

Janet led the team in singing hymns and praise to the Lord as they traveled the road from Clanston to their destination. Her eager enthusiasm and excitement inspired the others.

Forty-five minutes later, the van approached the town they had feared so much.

The muscles in Anthony's chest tightened. "Who is that man standing at the off ramp?"

"Is he thumbing his way into town or out of it?" Janet asked.

"Now he's standing in the middle of the road," Chris said. "Maybe he's just loony."

With a flash of armor, the man took the position for battle. A long, shining sword in his right hand aimed at them.

The hair rose on the back of Anthony's neck. "I'm not suited for battle. Is anyone else suited for battle?"

"No," Abby said.

"No," the others repeated.

"Please Lord, protect us," Anthony cried. "I don't dare take my eyes off the road."

"Remember the army coming with us, no need to panic," Michael reminded them. "Look out the side windows and drink in the sight of them."

"*Stop,*" the Elite Commander said in an audible voice. *"Pick the man up, and take him with you."*

"Yes, Lord." Anthony stepped on the break. "But we don't even know who he is."

"I thought you guys would never get here," the man said, as he opened the door of the minivan. "I have been waiting for you."

"Waiting? For us?"

"Yes, I'm Daniel Samuels. The Lord sent me to help you."

Then Anthony saw his name *Emissary* in the right shoulder. "Oh! You are the one we have been waiting for. Jump in and we'll continue the trip."

~*~

"Heh, heh," Botis chuckled. "We've got them, My Prince."

Apollyon responded with an evil smile and raised his leathery wings. "Get ready. The enemy is approaching. Crash, kill, and destroy everything."

"But My Prince, look ahead." Malphas gestured frantically. "We cannot attack, they have come ready for battle, and they outnumber us."

"Yes, look at that," Abdiel said with a curse. "The Elite Commander is leading them and they are protected by the heavenly army's shield. If we attack, we will be the ones massacred, not them."

Apollyon lowered his wings in defeat. "Stand down for now. Stand down. We will fight another day." He looked around at his men. "We need a new strategy."

"My Prince the shield of the army is making a circle around them. The light is shining so bright; it hurts my eyes," Samaels complained.

"Step back, all of you," Apollyon directed his warriors. "Hide in the blissful darkness behind us."

Anger filled the evil squad as the demons hid and watched the army of God pass by.

They gnashed their teeth.

Their eyes flashed with hatred.

~*~

Stand firm and be ready in case the enemy

attempts to strike. I can see their evil eyes hidden in the darkness," the Elite Commander told the Heavenly army. "They thought they were going to trap the team again.

"How naïve of them," Archangel Gabriel said.

~*~

Although Anthony felt the darkness engulfing the town he was no longer afraid. The team plans to visit Josh and Big Jax came by the orders of, and with blessing of, their King.

In less than five minutes they arrived at the Slattersville closed security prison, and since Tadd James had recently transferred there, it was easy for them to enter and call for the inmates they wanted to see.

Josh and Big Jax were soon delivered to the guest room where the inmates could freely mingle with their visitors.

The moment Michael saw his former cellmates he put one arm around each, and gave them both a side hug. "Josh, my man. Big Jax, I am so glad to see you again."

"I wasn't sure you would be able to come," Big Jax said."

"Yes. I'm blessed to be able to be here with all the members of our precious team. At last we can all be together."

"Tadd James," exclaimed Josh. "I didn't know you were part of the team."

"Yes, I am, and I've been transferred here. The two of you will not be alone at this prison."

"Guess that means I have to apologize for knocking you down." Big Jax shook his head and gave an exaggerated sigh.

That broke the ice as everyone chuckled.

"We've been impatiently waiting for the arrival of the Emissary to give us further instructions," Anthony said. "But God's timing is perfect and here he is."

Daniel Samuels nodded toward one of the prisoners. "I've already met Josh."

"Yes, Daniel visited me earlier and told me I would be getting a new cellmate. Nice to see you again, Brother. As you can see, my new cellmate arrived, and I'm not dead yet."

After making sure Josh and Big Jax knew all the other members of the team, Anthony deferred to the Emissary. "Daniel, it is your call, but could you give us the message from the Lord at this time?"

Daniel took a deep breath. "First, it's confession time."

Anthony nodded in sympathy when Daniel mentioned he had a confession. After all, the team had recently messed up royally.

"I was once a young man, and like all of you, my heart was filled with the fire of the Spirit. Like all of you I was eager to serve." He closed his eyes a moment.

"I had a great family, a wife, a daughter and a son." He continued.

"God blessed my efforts. I was an international leader for many countries, including Japan. God performed miracles of all kinds through me. He gave me the gifts of the Spirit for Revelation, Power, and Inspiration. I was blessed beyond words."

Daniel shook his head. "The problem came when I began to think I was unstoppable. Somehow along the road, I got lost and let pride fill my heart."

"Like us," Anthony said.

Daniel nodded. "Then, I lost my family and everything I loved. That's when I abandoned the ministry I was given and put down my sword. I was blinded for many years."

He pointed at Anthony. "When I saw you coming into this town. I knew you were up against the same thing I had gone through. But even then, I wasn't sure I wanted to get involved."

He paused and looked over the group. "I resisted the thought of getting back into the fight. But when you went into that room, I heard the order given by the ruler of the town."

No one made a sound. Daniel had the attention of the whole team. Anthony wasn't sure anyone was even breathing at that moment.

"You were lead into a trap without knowing it. And at that moment, I started to feel again. My heart burned within and tears filled my eyes. I asked the Lord for forgiveness and He freely embraced me. That's when. God gave me specific instructions for all of you."

Anthony could feel the tension leave the room as Daniel indicated he would soon deliver the Lord's message for them.

"First, I needed to rescue you from that evil trap, because there was no way you could do it on your own. Not without more training. The dark powers were too strong. I could not rescue you by myself, either. It took the order of the Elite Commander for His army, to join forces with me and finish that battle before it was too late."

"Can you tell us what happened?" Anthony asked. "We have no idea. Because, by then we were injured and blinded."

"With thousands of blades from the army combined with my lighting sword you were rescued that day with one single blow. Then the Lord instructed me to tell you everything that had happened."

Anthony raised his hands. "Praise the Lord. I only wish we could have actually seen it."

"Dark times are approaching along with an

imminent war against the forces of darkness. But you are not ready."

"How well we know it," Anthony agreed. "We got the message, loud and clear, during our defeat that day. We figured we needed to put in more prayer time."

"As I indicated, you also need more training. None of you understand the implications of the powers you've been given and some of you have not yet received your powers."

"I am sure you are right."

"The enemy has joined forces and is ruling this town. You might not have seen it, but they were ready to crush you when you entered their domain today."

"Yikes," said Janet.

"God gave them a glimpse of the army traveling with you. And now I am here to instruct and train you on each power." Daniel looked at the two inmates. "Josh and Big Jax have one final task here at the prison before they are released."

Big Jax's eyes widened. "Me too? Are you saying I will be released?"

"Yes, the Lord will release both of you to receive the training you will need for the larger war. But first, you two still have some battles to fight in the prison. Be watchful and be ready. It is not going be an easy one."

"Whatever the Lord asks of me, I will do," Josh said.

"Josh, your biggest trial lies ahead." Daniel nodded his head toward Big Jax as he continued to address Josh. "You have to trust each other. The only way you can win this battle is to become one with Big Jax. The two of you will be partners in this fight."

Chapter 9

Before the team said good bye they prayed with Josh and Big Jax. Then once again they all loaded up in the mini-van.

"Where to?" Anthony asked the Emissary.

"If it isn't too much out of your way to drop me off at my humble abode, I think I could rustle up a bite for all of you."

"Sounds good." Abby rubbed her stomach. "I seem to have a ferocious appetite lately."

"Erin, what did you do to her?" Janet asked with a giggle.

"I see how you are." Erin grinned. "You think you can blame me for everything now."

"That's what friends are for," Janet retorted.

"Turn right up here," the Emissary said.

"Wow," Janet said. "You have a huge and beautiful house."

"Thanks, Janet. I built it during the time I had become filled with pride. I thought it would impress my family. But, in spite of all my efforts, I lost them."

"I didn't think there was anything this picturesque in Slattersville," Anthony said. "How big is this place?"

"Not so big. Just ten acres. It was undervalued when I got it. The area had deteriorated and the property values fell. The former owner was behind in his payments. The way it ended up I only had to pay the back taxes."

"Even with the fence I don't see how you keep it so nice living so near a town like Slattersville."

"Yes, it's true that Slattersville is a rough area. The security system helps," the Emissary said with a droll smile. He punched in a code and the gate opened so they could enter.

"It's like a park back here," Sandra said. "It's so peaceful. I love it."

"Did you build the patio yourself?" Tadd gestured to the expansive brick surface.

"Actually, I did. After I dropped out of God's army I bought this land and started working it. I hoped it would keep my mind occupied."

"I'd say lugging those bricks would numb your brain instead," Tadd said.

The Emissary laughed at that remark. "Come on inside, and I will give you a tour."

They followed him past the four-car garage and up the steps to the front porch of the three story mansion and entered the double doors of the entry. A second set of doors showed how security conscience Daniel had been when he planned the house.

"Do you have an alarm system on both sets of doors?" Anthony asked.

"Smart lad." the Emissary stepped through the second entrance. "Come on in. I'll show you around downstairs." He waved his arm toward the grand oak staircase. "Then you can feel free to explore the upstairs on your own while I fix lunch."

"Wow, Erin," Abby said to her friend. "Get a load of the laundry room and kitchen. I can't believe Daniel's wife would give up something like this."

"She was spooked by this town. After I left God's army, she couldn't stay here. So she never gave this house a chance."

"I'd love to work in this kitchen. Can I help you fix lunch?"

"Me too," said Erin. "Tell us what you have in mind and show us where you keep everything."

Since the women got stalled in the kitchen, the men wandered through the rest of the house.

Anthony was impressed with the mixture of tile and hard wood flooring and the white marble wainscoting. He climbed the stairs to the upper levels and looked into each of the rooms. *What does one man do with nine bedrooms and five baths?*

When he was back on the lower level he wandered into the kitchen. He found Erin and

Abby busy cutting up a salad. Janet and Sandra stood near the stove.

"Can I help you with anything?" Anthony asked.

"How about calling the others together," Daniel said. "We can eat out on the patio."

It didn't take long for the crew to gather. While they ate, Daniel asked each of them questions. He seemed to want to get to know them on a personal level and had a way of putting everyone at ease.

"I have a mission to work with you all, and I am determined to accomplish it, but I cannot do it alone," Daniel finally said.

Along with the others, Anthony fixed his eyes on Daniel.

"As I told you earlier, I've been appointed to train you in the ways of the Lord's army. He has given each of us spiritual gifts and powers. I know this will be overwhelming and at first it might seem a little difficult for some of you."

"Just know we are grateful that you agreed to instruct us," Anthony said.

"I have another confession, though. I've been trying to figure out how this training was going to be accomplished and where." Daniel's eyes widened as if the thought had just occurred to him. "After seeing you all together. Is there any better place to train you than here at my humble residence?"

The team members all laughed.

Anthony clapped Daniel on the shoulder. "If that is God's command, I am sure the team will agree on it."

"For sure," the others said in unison.

"I'm sure now, that this was His plan all along when he let me build this place. Our first mission is that we all dedicate some alone time with God. Then we will meet here as soon as the Lord tells me He is ready for us to begin.

Chapter 10

The next day, Anthony drove the five people who lived in Michel and Deborah's house to New Hope Trinity. And for the first time since his conversion, Michael was able to attend a Sunday church service.

Michael was sad that he'd never had a chance to meet the Pastor Joe. While the other's mourned, however he rejoiced to be sitting on the comfortable pew beside the wife of his heart.

Pastor Joe must have been a wonderful man the way everyone in the congregation praised his memory.

To further celebrate Michael's homecoming Deborah had invited the team members to their place after church to share a simple meal.

He was glad to help her because he was so sick of the prison meals. He loved to use the gas grill and mixed his own hamburger patties with a special marinate recipe.

When the others had called earlier and offered to bring something Deborah had taken the opportunity to discover the picnic food specialties of each one.

Janet had a secret recipe for baked beans she

had inherited from her mother. And as Michael grilled outside, the baked beans bubbled on the counter in a crock pot.

Sandra said her potato's salad was the best in Ohio.

Abby's claim to fame was the way she presented various kinds of fresh vegetables. "Erin will help me fix a salad," she'd said.

"I crank a mean tub of homemade ice-cream. I can bring my ice-cream freezer," Tadd offered.

"Since I used to work with children, I developed some great cookie recipes," Chris said. "That should go good with Tadd's ice-cream."

That left Anthony and he laughed at himself. "In self-defense Becky never let me cook. But I make a great pot of coffee. How about if I furnish the drinks. After all, what's a picnic without soda pop?"

Sure enough, Erin and Abby's salad looked too pretty to disturb. But after the prayer for the meal, hunger kicked in and the team filled their plates.

It was interesting to see and taste what everyone else had brought.

Anthony had risen to the occasion and got a half of a wooden wine barrel at the Home Depot store. He'd filled it with crushed ice to chill the variety of canned pop.

"I never did tell you how impressed I was that

you sacrificed your Porsche and bought that minivan," Janet said.

"Remember the first time you took me to New Hope?" Anthony asked. "I was chagrined when you insisted on driving your Honda Civic instead of riding with me. Then I thought about Becky wondering when I would start earning my keep again. That is the first time it occurred to me to trade it in on something more practical."

"So what does she think about it?"

"Well, it was mid-August before I got it and we haven't seen each other since then."

Janet poked him in the ribs. "Surely you've talked to her on the phone."

"Don't be so hard on him," Tadd said. "It must be hard to have a long distance relationship."

Michael rolled his eyes. "Tell me about it."

"I plan to call Becky tonight and tell her I will be in Ohio next week-end. It will be easier to talk to her in person. She doesn't even know I passed the state boards."

"Congratulations. The rest of us didn't know that either. You didn't tell any of us."

Anthony shrugged. "Seems there were always more pressing matters to discuss with everyone."

~*~

"My Prince, I am happy to report, this time things are going according to plan," Botis said as he approached Apollyon. "Perdix and

Succumbus have completed the job with that old laggard, Pastor Joe. The old man is no longer in the land of the living, and the battle for the people he influenced is ours."

"Great job." Apollyon smiled evilly. "We can now destroy that little shack they call their church. Get to work right away on the next phase."

"Yes, My Prince. I will do it. But, there is something else I need to inform you about, My Prince."

"What is it now, Botis?"

"I am hearing some rumors among the evil commanders."

"Spit it out already," Apollyon snapped.

"We've detected signs of lights flickering about our old defeated friend, Daniel Samuels."

"You don't say. Have you checked it out further?"

"Yes My Prince. There are rumors their Elite Commander has renamed him *the Emissary*. That does not sound good at all. He was a worthy adversary, and we do not want to fight him again."

"What are you worried about? We defeated him once. We'll defeat him again." Apollyon's eyes flashed. "But keep a close watch on his movements. We cannot afford any mistake this time."

"Yes, My Prince." Botis bowed.

"What about the other job? Are we ready for the hit?"

"Yes, My Prince. We are set to go five days from now."

"You better be sure it goes off without a hitch."

"No worries, My Prince. I am working directly with Koroshiya san, the Assassin and the cruel Pat Williams. There are none better for the job than those two."

Apollyon frowned. "Good, make no mistake this time, whoever fails will see my other face."

Chapter 11

"Stop whining." Beth Cooper stood over Robert Milton with hands on hips. "Why don't you act like a man? It's not like you loved him all that much."

Her words cut through Robert like a knife. He frowned. "Of course, I loved my father."

"Oh, right. You were always complaining about things he wanted you to do, always cursing and wishing him dead. Now that he's gone you're acting like a baby."

He turned away from her. "Can't you understand that I'm hurting, Beth? He was the only living family I have left."

She punched him in the arm. "Oh! And what am I? Am I nothing to you?"

"Of course, you are important to me," Robert lied.

"I'm tired of not being able to go out in public with you. I've been hiding for almost a year, and have had to act like a ghost. It gets so old pretending that we don't know each other."

He hung his head. "Yes, Beth, you are right. I am sorry. I just hate all of this."

"You hate what, Milton?" Her voice dripped ice. "How dare you? What are you talking about?"

Robert cringed inside. This woman could do his reputation serious damage. He put his arms around her "I'm sorry, Babe. It is not you. I didn't make myself understood."

"I know I am not your wife, but being your lover, should give me some rights. Doesn't it?"

He needed comfort and nuzzled her cheek. "Beth, darling. I do love you. In fact, I am crazy about you. You know that, right?"

"I guess," Beth said with a sigh.

"What I hate is this church thing. I never wanted to be a holy acting type of guy."

"Yeah, if it wasn't for the money—"

"That's right. When my father called me to assist him with the finances of the church, I was happy because that gave me some extra money right about the time I met you."

"So now that he's gone, why can't we live a little? After all, he's been gone four weeks."

Robert took a deep breath trying to hold back his anger. "Because the money isn't in the bag yet."

"Sure. But, that just means we still have to lay low. Not that we can't have some fun. Right?"

"Of course, we can have fun." He hugged her again and rubbed his hands up and down her back. "But I hate having to go to church and pretend to be a pastor. What was Dad thinking? Don't get me wrong, I love the benefits. The public admiration is sweet. I have a decent income with good financial prospects." He nuzzled her cheek. "And I have you. The best thing of all is you."

"Yeah, Babe," Beth said. "I will take your sorrow and pain away. Relax, sweetheart. Let me get you something to drink. Hey let's do something new. What if I call one of my friends to keep us company? Ever tried a three-some?"

Jealous as Beth was, he'd never expected her to suggest anything like this. "You sure know how to light up my day."

"Tell me what you want, and I'll just make a call. There's a new girl at the club that you might enjoy. Let me surprise, you Babe."

Ten minutes later, the new girl knocked on his door. She was very beautiful and appeared to be of Latin origin. Her blond hair attracted him, and he guessed her age to be about nineteen. As soon as Robert saw her, he was caught in her trap.

This is the kind of life I love and I cannot allow anyone to know about it, ever. I'll have the best of both worlds.

The not-so-reverend enjoyed spending Sunday night at Beth's place and letting the new girl pleasure him.

~*~

"We are doing a great job," said Succumbus, a beauty, appearing in her normal form, with dark eyes, dark hair, as well as a very dark heart.

A resourceful demon she presented in other forms as the situation required. In the past when she had attacked Abby, she had morphed from a nurse disguise into an ugly haggard being.

In her wolf form she could present as many as four-heads.

And when her rage took her out-of control, as when she'd confronted Janet at Pastor Joe's house, she presented as a spinning tornado which showed her belligerent attitude.

She glanced at her buddy Perdix with a wicked grin. "Our master will be pleased with the results this night."

But no smile crossed the Demon of Despair's lips. Small in stature, Perdix's eyes remained cast down, sobs emanating from his throat even when dancing with supposed glee at Succumbus's words.

Anger surged through him as the sound of evil laughter surrounded him. But he dared not tell Succumbus.

~*~

Three weeks ago God had told Becky it was time to move to Ohio. But it was still a struggle.

"New York has always been my home," she'd prayed. "I know where everything is, and I love that. I can go anywhere at any time to get anything I need. My friends are here, my co-workers, my job, our new church, Ben's friends and the school."

And although God had been working with her she knew this was going to be a very difficult change.

"I have to stop waiting for Anthony to let me know what he's found out before I notify the doctor's office. Should I tell them now, or wait? I think, I should, at least, start giving him some small pieces of information, since I still don't know the actual date he will be ready for us."

"Mom, are you talking to yourself?" Ben asked.

"Yeah. Sorry, I was thinking out loud." Becky said. "But, guess what? Daddy is coming to New York for the weekend."

"Yay," Ben said. "Super."

"Would you like to help me start packing?"

"I thought Dad was coming here. Why are we packing?"

"Don't you think it is time we moved to Ohio to be with him?"

"Yes, it's time," Ben agreed. "Maybe I can go to a real school when we get to Ohio."

"Oh, Ben. Haven't you enjoyed the home

school program we've got? Pastor Good highly recommended it."

Ben shrugged. "It's alright. I guess."

"Here's the thing, Ben. I applied online to get my Esthetician license transferred to Ohio and I just got the information I need. So while I wait for a job I'd planned to continue to teach you."

"Okay."

"We can do your studies in the mornings, and you can have your evenings free the same as if you were going to public school."

"Where will we live?" Ben seemed to lose interest in the discussion about his schooling.

Becky started laughing. "I think we will live in the little apartment with Daddy."

"At Mrs. Deborah's house?"

"Uh huh," Becky said. "God has been working on my pride."

"Cool."

"So the point is we have to pack up our things. I'm thinking we should store them at Aunt Janet's house for a while. Because it is time to put this house on the market."

"Why can't we just take our stuff to Ohio?"

"Because we don't have any place to store our things there, and her house is available. At least for now."

"Whatever."

"We can take our clothes. And I'm sure a few

of your toys will fit in the little guest house. So pick out your two favorites."

"Oh, Mom," Ben whined. "Only two?"

Chapter 12

Concerned about the troubled atmosphere at New Hope Trinity Church, Abby arrived early for the Wednesday evening service. She settled into an out of the way pew and bowed her head. "Lord, I know there is something fishy behind Pastor Joe's death, please guide me in figuring out where the problem is coming from. Help our congregation heal from this tragedy."

There was no answer from the Lord. Instead, Janet, Chris, and Sandra walked toward her.

"Are you ok, Abby? God told us you had come to the church early and sent us to check up on you."

"Yes, I'm fine. I just don't understand what's going on, and it's upsetting. I was praying and asking for guidance. Sending the three of you here to be with me must be His answer."

"I expect He sent us as reinforcements," Janet said, "so let's hold hands and pray together."

One by one the four team members pleaded with God to show them how to help this congregation they had come to love. They asked Him to help them discover what had really happened to Pastor Joe.

"I have a special assignment for you," the Elite Commander said. "I will divide you into pairs for the job. Be careful, but do not fear. Remember I have given you this work and I am with you."

Peace filled Abby's heart as the Lord spoke.

"I have opened your eyes to see what is going on. Chris and Sandra, keep your eyes on Reverend Milton tonight. Abby and Janet, you two watch the others in the congregation and notice anything different in the building during the service."

"I feel better knowing what direction to take this evening," Abby said. "Since Janet will be up front at the organ, I will stay at the back.

"Sandra and I can stand on opposite sides of the sanctuary, but close enough that we can watch the podium. That way the whole place should be within our view."

"That's a great plan." Abby nodded. "By the way, did you know Reverend Milton isn't going to preach tonight?"

Janet's eyes widened. "Why not?"

"The reverend is so torn up over his father's passing that he has delegated the sermons to Rick Watson for the rest of this month. He's been an elder and assistant pastor here at Trinity for many years. Have you met him yet?"

"Do you mean Brother Rick?" asked Chris.

"Yes, the very same. Good, you all have met

him, then."

"I've met him too," said Sandra. "He will do well. He's a good man with a heart for the Lord."

"I see the reverend is arriving now." Abby gestured toward the doorway. "Since the Elite Commander put the four of us on watch tonight, we can be sure something is going to happen, but what, is yet to be revealed."

~*~

Reverend Robert Milton took a seat near the podium with Rick Watson. He didn't have plans to assist that evening, but he wanted to sit where he could see and listen to Janet as she played the organ. When she laid hands on the instrument, he felt at peace. It was as if she had an angel's touch.

Soon the other parishioners began arriving for the evening service.

Janet took her place and the organ music wafted through out the sanctuary.

Reverend Milton could not help but smile at the joy he felt at that moment. Something indescribable flowed over and through him along with the melody from the organ.

But as soon as she stopped playing, the reverend knew his heavy burden would return. He would be back to his normal feeling of anger and hatred.

It was a good thing he was accomplished at

concealing his real feelings. He should be. He'd had lots of practice.

~*~

As Janet played the organ, Sandra stood on the right side of the sanctuary, Chris took the left, and Abby remained on guard at the main entrance.

Suddenly, Sandra waved her hands. Janet figured the others in the congregation would think she was following the rhythm of the hymn "Amazing Grace".

But Janet knew Abby was sending a signal. She became alert when she realized Abby wanted the other three team members to pick up on the dark presence on the second bench from the front row where five young women sat. She knew one of the women as Nina Patel. Another was Beth Cooper.

Janet noticed a dark being sitting between the two young women. As God cleared her vision, she could see the dark being resembled a very attractive woman. But the weird thing was the powerful aura coming from her stretched out and almost covered the whole pew. She must be a very powerful demon. The problem was Janet couldn't discern which of the two young women the demon was influencing.

The music finished, and Janet stepped away from the organ.

As soon as the music stopped another dark aura appeared and seemed to radiate from Reverend Milton.

A very rattled Janet got down from the podium. She could feel her body tense and prepare for battle. Surely not in the church. She glanced around, fearing for the other members in the building.

"Hold it. It is not time for battle yet. You will observe, but not fight tonight," the Elite Commander calmed her heart.

Janet trembled as she watched the darkness grow, almost covering the entire church. It was no longer simply the dark presence radiating from Reverend Milton, and from between Nina and Beth.

And the troubling thing was that it still wasn't clear from which of the girls the dark aura was coming.

It was a strong and overpowering presence like nothing Janet had yet encountered. Was it the same force that had defeated the team in Slattersville? That encounter had demoralized them and she had a feeling they were not yet ready to fight this enemy.

She could hardly concentrate on the message from Brother Rick. "Sorry, Lord," she prayed silently.

"Stay alert," her Elite Commander said.

The darkness in the church faded somewhat as Brother Rick used the Savior's name over and over in his message. But the shadow still hovered over Robert Milton and the young women in the second pew.

At last the church services finished without further incident. The four team members hugged one another without saying a word. It was not yet time to share their discovery.

Chapter 13

"Boss."

"Dragon."

"Big Jax."

"Boss, boss, boss."

Josh wanted to tie something around his head to block the noise reverberating throughout the cell block.

"The other inmates cannot know about my change of allegiance," Big Jax told Josh. "The timing has to be just right. I know it's going to be complicated, but we need to be very careful."

"Yeah. You sure didn't like it when I changed over." Josh shrugged. "So what else is new?"

"There is more going on this time than what you can see, and I don't know if you understand the situation we're in."

"Then tell me about it."

"It's not just because that was you and now it's me. I've been pretty high up in the leadership of the organization for years. Not only in the towns of Slattersville and Clanston, but other places as well."

"I'd kind of gathered that."

"Josh, I will try to protect you as much as I

can, but it's important that you listen to me."

"Of course. I get that. And while I may not understand everything, the Lord is on our side. So I'm not really worried," Josh said. "But, I'll confess the way all the other prisoners are yelling out your name is freaking me out."

Just then a guard stood by their cell gate. "You need anything sir?" He looked at Big Jax.

The giant of a man shook his head at the guard as a refusal, without saying a single word.

"Sorry, to disturb you, sir." The guard turned on his heel and he left.

"What was that all about?" Josh whispered.

"Like I told you before, there is more to this place than what you can see."

Josh trembled involuntarily as he felt a strong evil presence approaching their cell. The door opened, and a dark shadow entered.

A giant snake resembling an Anaconda slid into the room and ended up where Josh and Big Jax stood beside the bunks.

The snake raised its red head and focused piercing dark eyes on Josh. The creature opened its mouth, and venom dripped from its fangs.

"Sorry, boss," the voice of Viper hissed. "I should have gotten rid of this rat earlier. Shall I take care of it now?"

"Wait."

The snake flung is large body upward toward

Josh.

"God help me," Josh cried.

"*Do not fear, I am with you.*"

At the same moment the Elite Commander spoke to him, Josh felt himself transformed into a warrior with a long Messer sword in his hand. The sword flamed fire, and Josh planted his feet apart like a warrior ready for battle.

~*~

Big Jax glanced at Josh's right shoulder and saw he'd received his new name *The Polyglot.* Big Jax was pleased for his fellow team member.

His muscles twitched to join the fight, but a dark force hindered him from moving to help. Was he so soon overpowered by the forces of evil? Big Jax watched helplessly as Viper went for the kill.

Polyglot took his first swing at the snake.

Viper *the snake* twisted and avoided the attack. His jaws twitched. His fangs dripped venom.

Big Jax, *the Decipher,* knew Viper, his former underling, was getting ready to use venom, his secret weapon, to deliver a lethal hit.

Overpowering the forces that had held him back, the *Decipher* managed to move and grab the head of the big Anaconda with his bare hand and stopped Viper's momentum.

"I said, wait. That means not yet," Big Jax

roared. "Don't you realize we might need him later? Are you defying me?"

Viper the snake slithered backwards. "Sorry, boss, I ain't hear ya." He bowed his head to the ground in submission.

"OK, but you still have a lot to learn." Big Jax's voice was gruff as he tried to conceal his new allegiance. "Other than this mishap, are we ready, Snake?"

"Yes, boss, almost ready." Viper's voice seemed thoughtful, and somewhat different. Had he noted something off about his boss?

"Almost?" Big Jax kept his countenance firm. "Go then."

Viper gave his boss one last look with unblinking reptilian eyes and left.

~*~

He'd ended up in the corner of the room, but Josh had been ready to continue. Of course, he'd been afraid to let up. And what if it was his time to go? Or what if he'd misread God's signal. All kinds of thoughts ran through his mind. He hadn't seen Big Jax's armor. *I know he's a very strong dude, but did he really just use his bare hands?*

"We could have won the fight." Josh's bravery came back with a vengeance. "We could have defeated Viper."

"Yes, Josh, I know, but this is not the time. As

I said before, we need to be very careful, otherwise, I am afraid that we will not survive. Do you remember what I told you about my dreams?"

"Yes, I do."

"I don't want to be a disappointment to my new Leader," *the Decipher* said.

A few minutes later, Tadd James showed up. "I heard about a disturbance. What's up, guys? Is everything alright in here?"

Josh shared his aborted battle with Viper who had taken the form of a giant snake.

"But he is a human. Was that the first time you'd seen him teamed up that closely with a demon?"

"That's right," Josh said. "And another thing, I think some of the guards are on the side of evil. One came to see if Big Jax needed anything special."

Tadd's eyes widened. "Are you kidding me?"

"He's not kidding." Big Jax went on to share who he was in reality. He went into more detail for Tadd, since he'd never been part of it.

Big Jax explained how he'd controlled the gangs and everything in the town from within the prison itself. Being incarcerated was no detriment to the evil plans. He emphasized the need for precautions and smooth talk whenever and wherever Tadd found himself in the prison.

"I mean it. Do not trust anyone in here. Not even the other guards."

"Okay," Tadd said. "But it's really sad news. It really burns me whenever I hear about crooked law enforcement."

"Make no mistake. A big storm is coming, and we need to be ready for it. If they find out about my new identity before Josh and I get out of here, we will be in great danger."

"I will continue to pray for guidance," Tadd said.

"As will we," Josh agreed.

~*~

That evening there was a big commotion just outside of Slattersville. Someone was throwing a party.

Koroshiya San observed the gangs celebrating the arrival of, Big Jax, the boss, back into town.

It wasn't a problem that he was moving to the prison rather than the town proper, because Big Jax and his second in command, Viper Chambers, controlled everything. They controlled the town, the prison, and distribution through the grapevine, all from inside the prison.

And Koroshiya San, a tall and strong American with Japanese origin, was third in command after Viper. As their liaison outside of the prison, he was always seeking to honor his gang name *The Assassin.*

Koroshiya San planned to excel and show the boss how well the business was going and how profitable he had kept it. Surely he would be properly rewarded.

"We must work even harder now," he said.

"Yes, sir," his underlings all replied at once.

Now that the boss is finally here, should I visit him or just wait for our plan to work out? Koroshiya San remembered he'd been told to wait. *Okay, I will wait.*

He raised his head as Pat Williams, Koroshiya San's right hand, and best worker, approached. She was a cruel and despicable woman, according to the underlings. They all feared her and trembled when her commands were directed their way.

"Boss," she said. "We have new people coming into town. Should we check them out?"

He shook his head. "Other tasks have urgent priority for now, but if they show up again, I want you to find out who they are, where they go and what they are doing in my town,"

"Yes, sir." She bowed, giving proper reverence to his position and then left.

Chapter 14

For years, Daniel Samuels had been like a shadow and no one had paid much attention to him. He'd explored Slattersville with confidence. But since he'd recommitted his life to the Elite Commander, he became more aware of his surroundings and something itched the back of his mind.

He knew this place was an evil stronghold. He'd been reminded of it when he'd recently observed the demon influence at the prison. But had it always reached this far? He felt a dark presence as he approached what he'd long considered a fairly neutral area. He may need to find a new walking path.

Daniel approached a car parked along the road just ahead. A tall and muscular man stepped out. He seemed familiar, like someone from Daniel's past.

As he got closer the man turned and faced him. "Out jogging, old friend?"

When Daniel heard the voice, he recognized his old friend Koroshiya San. His expression indicated this was not a friendly visit.

"I've heard you have new friends," Koroshiya

San told him. "That is not good. We allow no new people in the neighborhood but our own. You must get away from them."

After he had delivered the message the Japanese American got back into his car. Pat Williams sat in the passenger seat. As Koroshiya San drove past Daniel, that old familiar face blew him a kiss from the car.

Things must be speeding up around here for Koroshiya San and Pat Williams to come to deliver a message to me in person.

"Dear Lord," Daniel prayed. "The storm is coming, and we are not yet ready. Your team has not even begun their training."

~*~

Meanwhile at the prison, Viper watched Big Jax and Josh amble into the patio where the inmates were allowed some free time.

Viper eyed the empty bench in front of him, but the two cellmates sat in a corner near the fence and some of the others.

The inmates sitting with Viper began to chatter. "Looks like the boss has a new puppet," one murmured."

More comments were made which Viper did not appreciate. In spite of the order of his boss to wait. And especially since the boss had said they might need the rat, the snake was blinded with jealousy.

It's time to step on the throat of that rat. Without saying anything to the others, Viper stood and headed toward Josh.

~*~

Josh knew Big Jax needed to continue to blend in and put the other prisoners at ease. So he had no problem when Big Jax talked with the inmates sitting on his other side, and paid no attention to him.

Hearing a rustle from his right, Josh glanced over and then flinched away from the snake's big red head that had opened up and was lunging toward him.

"Time for battle," said the Elite Commander.

In a blink of an eye Josh was ready for the fight. He glanced at Big Jax but his cellmate was oblivious to what was happening right beside him.

The snake, threw its first strike, and hit Josh on the left arm. The other inmates noticed and formed a circle around the two gladiators.

"Fight. Fight. Fight," they chanted.

~*~

The chanting drew Big Jax's attention. He realized Josh was in great danger, but he couldn't move to help. *Should I just give in and blow my cover?* He questioned God in his mind.

"This is the polyglot's fight, he will take this one alone," replied the Elite Commander. "Stay and watch."

Both gladiators bled profusely. Big Jax glanced toward the guard towers. With the circle of inmates surrounding Josh and Viper, Big Jax was sure the guards were not able to see what was going on. Surely to them, everything looked normal.

The *polyglot* swung his sword, hitting the snake on the left side.

Then the Anaconda spewed out its fatal venom. "You are mine, rat, your time is over."

A combination of snake and human, Viper grabbed Josh by his left leg, throwing him on the ground. He stepped on Josh so hard his leg stopped bleeding for a second.

"It's not over yet." With an upward slash, the *polyglot's* sword pierced the reptile's head and blinded the Anaconda's right eye.

Pulling back its head, the Anaconda hissed in pain. If it were possible, the snake grew larger. Opening the ever widening mouth, Viper swallowed the polyglot. "Gulp. Gulp. Gulp."

"The battle is over," the crowd cheered. "The *snake* finally swallowed the rat."

A roar came from within the belly of the Anaconda. *"In the name of the Lord Jesus Christ, let me out."*

The Anaconda gagged and vomited out the polyglot.

The polyglot still held his sword and before he reached the ground he sliced the Anaconda's remaining eye, blinding it completely. "It's *you who is finished."*

The polyglot prepared his sword for the final blow when two guards grabbed him and threw him to the ground.

"Call the paramedics," one of the guards yelled. "These two men are severely injured."

Sammie, Viper's second in command, approached Big Jax. "Hey, Boss, the hit is tonight. Be ready."

Sammie glanced from Viper to Josh and left.

~*~

Tadd grabbed one side of Josh and another guard helped place him on a gurney.

"I got you covered, Josh," Tadd said. "Relax, I got you."

He glanced at the other inmates. "Nothing to see here. The show is over."

After the other guard helped load up viper, Tadd walked beside him and they wheeled both prisoners to the infirmary. Tadd made sure the two prisoners were not left close to one another.

After the doctor treated Josh, Tadd went to Big Jax's cell to inform him of Josh's condition.

"How is he?" Big Jax asked the moment Tadd entered the cell.

"He's not doing that well. His arm and leg

were severely hurt and are turning black. Viper is not able to see, but he is fine otherwise."

"Tadd to central," squawked the walkie-talkie.

"Copy central."

"Report to the office."

"Roger that." Tadd took off in a run.

When Tadd arrived at the office, he was surprised to see a visitor. Erin Ludwig came in a disguise as instructed by the Emissary. No one would know she was in town.

"Take me to Josh," she said. "The Lord sent words of healing for him. We need to hurry because the venom is about to kill him."

"Venom? What venom? What are you talking about?"

"Didn't you see the fight? He was up against a big snake and was bitten in his left arm and leg. The venom in his body is why he is turning black."

"But, how could you have known about it?" Tadd asked.

"I saw everything. The Lord showed it all to me on the way here, as if it were a movie."

Speechless, Tadd took the *mender's* hand and led her to the infirmary, where Josh lay.

"Josh." Erin rushed to his side. "The Lord sent me to heal you."

He didn't answer or acknowledge she was there.

She placed her hands over the black parts of his body and prayed earnestly for his healing.

Tadd marveled as Josh's arm turned pink and healthy. He glanced at Josh's leg. "It's still black!"

"Lord, I could use some help here." Erin said as she continued to massage Josh's leg.

"Would you look at that," Tadd said as the leg returned to Josh's normal flesh color and was healed.

"Well done, *Polyglot*." Mender gave him a final pat. "You put up a good fight. The Lord has rewarded you by restoring your health."

"Good job, Mender and Polyglot," the Elite Commander spoke in an audible voice.

For the first time Tadd James saw himself transformed into a warrior.

"Tadd, my faithful servant, you have *been* renamed the *Judge*. Honor the gifts and your new name," said the Elite Commander aloud.

"Judge, this next message is for your heart alone. The others need not be alarmed by the message. But you need to know the battle in this prison is not over. You need to stay in the cell with Josh and Big Jax tonight. The dark storm that you have heard about is coming."

"Lord, I will stay here as you have commanded," Tadd replied in his heart.

"The three of you will need to stick together to win this battle," the Elite Commander replied to the *Judge's* heart only.

~*~

Big Jax worried for Josh, but as he prayed for his cellmate's full recovery, he felt peace cover him.

Before long Tadd delivered Josh to the cell fully recovered and healed.

"So soon? How can this be? Josh, you were bleeding and severely hurt. How did you heal up so quickly? What happened?" Big Jax asked.

'God sent the *mender* to me in the infirmary."

Big Jax marveled. "Praise the Lord for her."

"I wish you could have seen his skin lose the awful purple-black color and return to his normal flesh tone. It was inspiring," Tadd said, "By the way, I have been given my new name today."

"Tell us what it is."

"*The Judge.*"

"Congratulations," said Big Jax."

"Did you learn the meaning of your name?"

"I am sure we will all learn more about our names as we get more training. But, guys, that is not all the news. The Lord said a dark storm is coming to the prison. He instructed me to stay here with the two of you. He says we need to stick together to survive the night."

"That's great," Big Jax said. "I received news while Josh was fighting that the hit is tonight. I wondered when the Elite Commander would reveal his plans."

"The hit?" Josh questioned.

"Yeah. What do you mean, what is this hit all about?" Tadd asked.

"My former team has organized a plan to get me, Viper and Sammie out of prison. And tonight is when it will go down."

"But what will actually happen?"

"The paperwork and everything is already taken care of. No one will know what happened here tonight and tomorrow everything will seem legal since the papers are already set in place."

"What about Josh?" Tadd asked. "What about the cell mates of the others on the rescue *hit?*"

"I can tell you this. The people breaking in tonight are very dangerous. Anyone standing in their way will perish," said Big Jax. "Koroshiya San and Pat Williams are leading the strike."

"Who are they?"

"They are very powerful. Just under Viper who is under me," Big Jax said. "Listen up Tadd, whatever happens tonight do not engage in battle. Do not get close to either of these two. That goes for you too, Josh."

"So why did our Elite Commander tell me to come here if I am just supposed to sit and twiddle my thumbs while the hit goes down?"

"I told you to avoid Koroshiya San and his

cohort Pat Williams. You will easily recognize them. Koroshiya San is totally bald with a short beard and dark, almost black eyes. He stands over seven feet in height, but if he is paired with a demon he may be as tall as nine feet."

"I guess I won't mess with him," Tadd said.

"Not you either, Josh," Big Jax warned.

"I hear you," Josh said.

"Alright. As for Pat Williams, do not be misled by her beauty, she is famous for her cruelty and despicable way of killing. She has short bobbed hair and deep green eyes. And by the way, she's known as the *Python*."

"Another snake." Josh shuddered.

"Make no mistake the Python is much more lethal than Viper."

Tadd James nodded. "Still, the Lord told me to stick with you two guys. At least, in case of battle, we will not be alone, we will be together."

"Do not engage," Big Jax said again. "Do not engage."

"Yeah, yeah. I hear you," Tadd said. "But listen. I have a plan."

Chapter 15

"When it is time to strike, you are to go with Koroshiya San," Apollyon said. "I need you to make sure there are no mistakes."

"Yes, My Prince." Botis took a step back and bowed. "Just as you wish."

As evening fell the Evil forces gathered and looked to their master for directions.

"It is time." Apollyon raised his leather wings in a powerful display. "Let's go to the prison and get my puppets out."

The cars moved toward their destination ready to crush and destroy everything in their path.

The evil forces followed the seven heavily armed vehicles carrying the most dangerous human beings into the town of Slattersville.

~*~

The Emissary, the long forgotten watcher of Slattersville, sat on the old familiar building where he'd watched over the town before his fall.

He gazed at the armored vehicles filled with the gang preparing to retrieve their leader. They had no idea that the dragon had changed sides and was now a saved one, called the Decipher.

"Do not engage, just watch," the Elite Commander said to the Emissary's heart. "I will let your vision penetrate the prison walls. Watch and hear this event as it unfolds."

The prison was engulfed in darkness, and the Emissary could only see three dim lights. The spirits of Tadd, Josh, and Big Jax, shone in the middle of the darkened gloom, and he could easily pinpoint their position.

When the vehicles arrived at the prison no guard attempted to stop them. They easily entered as if it was an everyday occurrence.

"Viper is at the infirmary," a guard said to Koroshiya San. "He was in a skirmish and is blinded. Sammie is with him, but he is not hurt."

Koroshiya San glanced at Pat Williams. "This may put a crimp in our plans. Go get them."

"Yes, Sir."

~*~

"How did you let this happen?" Pat Williams demanded as she leaned over the cot where Viper lay.

"Just shut up and get me out of here," Viper hissed.

"What use are you if you can't stay out of trouble?"

"I'll carry my boss out," Sammie said.

Sammie picked up Viper, and Pat Williams walked out beside them.

"Let's stop and get the Boss," said Viper.

"Koroshiya San is on his way to the cell now," Pat Williams said coldly. "We are to meet them at the front gate in five."

~*~

Tadd, Josh and Big Jax were waiting in the locked cell, when Koroshiya San arrived.

"What is this? The door was supposed to be open." He glared at Josh and then Tadd. "Three in one cell?" He pointed his head at Tadd. "You there, guard open the cell or I will kill the both of you."

Koroshiya San shifted his gaze to Big Jax. "Are you okay, Boss?"

"I am all right," Big Jax said. "But it looks like I'm not leaving."

Koroshiya San's face reddened as blue curses flew from his mouth. "What the heck is going on?" He pulled out his Japanese Honjo Masamune Sword ready to slice through the bars and kill them.

Tadd aimed his Glock 22 at Big Jax's temple. "This inmate is not leaving the prison alive."

Josh picked up a Smith & Wesson M&P 9 and pointed it right at Koroshiya San's heart.

Koroshiya San's eyes widened. "What went wrong, Boss?"

"Long story," Big Jax said with a defeated tone. "Just leave without me, for now."

"Sir, we only have two minutes. We must leave now," Kimura Ichi San said to Koroshiya San.

But Koroshiya San seemed stunned and didn't move.

"*Ikuzo.*" Kimura Ichi repeated himself in Japanese.

Then Koroshiya San backed away from the cell, not taking his eyes off of Big Jax until he reached the end of the aisle. He turned, walked out of the cell block, and out of the building.

Daniel watched as they left the prison grounds without a single incident, except for taking Viper and Sammie with them.

~*~

Big Jax knew he couldn't leave with Koroshiya San. He didn't dare. But no one could ever know what had really happened in his cell that night, or they would all be in great danger.

Tadd James was especially at risk from the authorities for lending his weapon to an inmate. But he was even more at risk from the evil forces for pointing his gun at Big Jax.

It was all part of the plan the three had concocted, and Big Jax had agreed it was the only way to convince his former gang to leave him there.

~*~

Koroshiya San rushed out of the building and

entered one of the cars, slamming the door behind him.

"What happened," Pat Williams asked. "Where is the Boss?" We don't really need these others without him, do we?"

"It was the weirdest thing. The cell was locked. Nothing went according to plan, and the Boss said he wasn't coming." Koroshiya San shook his head in bewilderment. Then he shared the full story with the other gang members in the car.

"Do you think he's changed sides?" Viper hissed.

"No way," Koroshiya San said. "He'd never give up his position. He worked hard to get to the top. Plus he looked as stunned as I felt."

"I don't know," Viper said. "He's been acting strange."

"Well, Viper. Just remember, you are no good to us blind," Pat Williams said.

"Let's take the snake to the witch doctor and get him fixed up," Sammie suggested.

Koroshiya San was frustrated. They'd managed to get these two out of the prison, but the most important one, the Boss didn't make it.

He'd wanted to talk to him. He was sure he could be more beneficial to the dragon than Viper. He'd hoped to rise to second in command.

They needed the Boss and would have to plan another hit soon.

~*~

"My Prince, I fear the dragon has switched his allegiance." Botis reported to Apollyon.

"What? Are you sure about it?"

"Not sure yet. I will find out, My Prince and let you know."

"So why do you suspect he has turned?"

"The dragon didn't slaughter that turn coat, Josh Pennington, when he turned at Clanston. He was mine, and I don't like to lose."

"He defied you in Clanston?"

"Don't take me wrong, the dragon managed to do plenty of damage, but someone moved Josh out of reach by sending him to Slattersville."

"I thought that was why you pulled strings to get the dragon moved to Slattersville as well. And as the cellmate of Josh, no less."

"That is correct My Prince. But Josh Pennington is still healthy. Nothing has happened since the dragon arrived. So I am going to investigate."

"Be sure that you bring back a report to me immediately."

"Yes, My Prince."

Chapter 16

"Welcome home Honey, how was your trip?" Becky greeted Anthony with a big hug and a kiss.

"The drive was long, and tiring, but worth every minute." Anthony grinned. "How I have missed you."

"Dad." Ben rushed down the stairs like a little storm and reached up his arms. "You're home."

Anthony leaned down and embraced his son.

Ben jumped on his daddy's neck to hug and kiss him.

"What's up, Buddy? You sure have a lot of energy tonight."

"He always has lots of energy," Becky said.

"I missed you, Dad. Hey, Dad. Can I see your armor? Your sword? Have you fought more battles? Has your boss—?

Anthony chuckled when Ben didn't give him a chance to slide a word in edgewise into the conversation.

"Slow down, Ben," Becky admonished her son.

"Okay, Mom." Ben looked up at Anthony and grinned.

"Hey, Slugger. Why don't we go outside and toss some balls? See if we can drain off some of that energy."

"Sure, Dad. But, guess what?"

"I'm listening. What do you have to say, buddy?"

"Mom says we are ready to move to Ohio. Whenever you say the word. I've even got my two toys packed already."

Anthony laughed. "Only two?"

"Yeah, Mom's orders. We have to store the rest."

~*~

Becky finished getting their meal prepared and then stood by the window. She enjoyed watching her two loves play in the yard.

It felt good to have her family together. But she still felt a twinge of apprehension when she thought about moving to Ohio. The whole idea was beyond her comfort level.

But she needed to obey the Lord's command. Besides, the thought that they would be together as a family comforted her.

"Hey, guys, dinner is ready, please come in."

Ben stayed wound up throughout the meal.

"Great meal," Anthony said. "I miss your cooking."

"Is that all you miss?" she teased.

"She doesn't cook like this when you're not

here," Ben said.

Becky kept reminding herself that they would have more good times like this when she moved. It was time.

After their late dinner, Anthony offered to put Ben to bed while she cleaned up. "I'll help you finish up when I come back downstairs," he promised.

Ben tugged on Anthony's hand. "You have to read me a story."

"Of course, little man. Of course." Anthony followed his son up the steps.

Becky hummed as she scraped the dishes and loaded the dishwasher. She was pleased when she heard her husband's footsteps coming down the stairs. It was time for them to be alone.

"I have great news," Anthony said as he stood behind her and nuzzled her neck. "I waited until I could tell you in person."

"What is it?"

"I've finally been able to set up my new office in Clanston, and I am working with some new clients already."

"That's great, Honey," Becky said. "I'm glad it's in Clanston. I Googled Slattersville, and that town doesn't seem to be a very desirable place to raise a family."

"You are right about that. But, that's not all my news. I have also rented a small apartment for the three of us, I am sure you will like it. It is in Clanston as well."

"You need to know that Ben and I are ready to go with you. I've already presented my resignation at work. And I've also applied to transfer my license to Ohio."

"Whoa. That is great news," Anthony said.

"It will take approximately four weeks for the process of transferring the license to take effect."

"So you can't begin the move for a month?"

"I didn't say that. I just can't get a job in Ohio for a month. Not in my chosen profession anyway.

"Don't worry about a thing. I'm sure I can keep you busy."

Becky giggled.

~*~

After their experience at the worship service last Wednesday night, the team realized they needed to continue paying close attention to everything that happened at New Hope Trinity Church since the death of Pastor Joe.

Although Reverend Robert Milton was still as handsome as ever, Janet had noticed the glow and charming presence he'd had in the past seemed to be vanishing. But maybe that was to be expected. After all, he was still mourning the death of his father.

Janet sensed there were more things

happening than what they could see on the surface. Something was behind all of this, but she could not figure it out just yet.

She felt especially at home in this church since the reverend had given her the opportunity to play the organ, and she wanted to discover what the problem was.

On Sunday, the team agreed to meet before the services and go over their concerns and then meet again afterwards and share anything they noticed in the evening service.

Chris was the first to voice his thoughts. "I don't have a problem with Reverend Milton delegating some of his duties and relying on the people in the congregation. Actually it's a wonderful idea because it gives opportunity to groom new leaders for the church."

Abby nodded. "Yes, he is a terrific man of God. He's here for most of the services. But I know he's still mourning for Pastor Joe, as we all are."

"At Wednesday's service we noticed the dark aura covering some of the young women," Sandra said. "However we couldn't determine who was being influenced. It should be helpful with more of us here this time. Please watch carefully tonight."

When the service was over, the team decided to go for dinner.

They all gathered together at the restaurant. Deborah, Michael, Janet, Abby, Tadd, Sandra, Erin, Chris. Everyone except Anthony, who'd gone to New York for the week-end.

Michael turned toward Janet. "I want you to know your music really blessed me this evening."

"And the message was wonderful as well," Deborah said. "I felt so blessed and I didn't notice anything out of line like I think you might have been looking for."

"You didn't see darkness hovering over Reverend Milton?" Sandra questioned.

"I noticed it last Wednesday when I finished playing the organ," Janet said thoughtfully. "I hadn't noticed it before then, and I can't say I noticed anything this morning either."

"That is why I hesitated to bring it up before now." Sandra sighed. "The dark presence is intermittent. I think I see it and then it is gone. I'd planned to check it out more before I mentioned anything."

"Anthony taught me that the darkness might indicate demon influence," Michael said. "Like when he first met me. So if any of us see anything that makes us suspect something like that we need to discuss it."

"But would a demon be inside the church?" Chris frowned as if the thought distressed him.

Which it likely did. "I'd hoped the sanctuary would always be a safe place."

"Don't forget the parable of the wheat and the tares." Sandra said. "Most people don't think about it, but demons can be inside the church as well. It takes the power of God to cast them out."

"I think you are right." Chris nodded. "Because this morning I saw something that might be a demon presence hovering around a young girl at the church. I watched her closely, and she was looking at Reverend Milton in a very strange way. It felt like lust and lewdness."

At this Abby flinched. "Are you referring to Beth Cooper, the woman who sat on the bench to my left?"

"No." Chris shook his head. "It was the girl next to her, the younger one. I've met Beth Cooper already and she seems nice enough."

"Oh, you must mean Nina Patel," Abby said.

"Yes." Chris agreed. "I believe that is her name."

"I know for a fact she has a crush on the reverend," Erin said. "Still, he is very conservative. As far as I know, he has never given her any encouragement."

"I hope not." Chris raised his brows at that. "I'd thought about speaking to him, but wanted to discuss this with the rest of you first."

"Obviously, we need to keep a close eye on

these three," Michael said in a subdued voice. "And we need to watch for any other suspicious activities at the church."

Chapter 17

Two months passed by without further incident or battles for the team. It was as if the evil forces had gone underground for the winter.

Light filled the sanctuary at New Hope Trinity. The team enjoyed the sermons given by Rick Watson. In fact he seemed to have taken over running the church.

Maybe it was just the calm before the storm, but Anthony was content. His family had settled into the apartment in Clanston, and he was still building his client base at his private lawyer's office.

Janet had quit working in the Clanston prison system and helped Anthony in his office. She promised to take over homeschooling Ben when Becky got her own dermatologist office established.

Becky's prospects were looking up because of Abby and Erin's connections at the hospital. They were able to introduce Becky to doctors who would be willing to refer patients to her.

And Sandra, with her vast experience, had helped locate Becky's office at the same building where she was established.

Michael and Deborah continued to grow together in the Lord.

Chris had taken a position as youth minister at the church.

And Tadd kept the team informed on the progress of Josh and Big Jax, while he gave the two inmates news on the individual team members.

That afternoon Anthony felt a crackling in the air.

"The darkest storm is approaching, and you all need to be ready. It is time to begin your training, Go to The Emissary, and take all the members of the team with you. He is waiting for you," said the Elite Commander.

God must have spoken to all the team members, because when Anthony called them, their responses were ready and strong in agreement.

~*~

After a long silence, words came to the Emissary.

"Josh has served his sentence, and I am getting Big Jax out of prison, as well," the Elite Commander said. "Now that the team can all be together, it is time to start their training. As you have already realized, you will host some of them at your house."

When the day of the release arrived, Daniel

Samuels waited for Josh and Big Jax at the gate. "You two are coming home with me."

"There is no place we would rather be right now," Big Jax said with a big grin.

The two former inmates followed The Emissary and walked to his home.

~*~

Of course the evil forces had not gone underground but were busy preparing to establish their rule over the towns Apollyon had assigned to them.

After the witch doctor healed Viper Chambers eyes, the snake took over position one, much to both Koroshiya San and Pat Williams's displeasure. Not that they would let Viper know their true feelings.

Koroshiya San pretended to be content being second in command. Pat Williams continued one position below him, followed by Kimura Ichi and Samuel Strong, better known as Sammie.

Although Viper Chambers was called Boss, there was one with a higher position. The Boss of the bosses. Nobody had seen his face. Nor did anyone know his real name. Therefore, the position of Boss of bosses was considered a myth by many.

But Viper Chambers had heard his voice when he'd spoken with Big Jax.

When Viper asked Big Jax about him, he'd

declared he only knew him by the title *The Lord of the Night.*

~*~

Sunday afternoon, Sandra called Chris. "Can we meet at New Hope Trinity Church in twenty minutes?"

"Sure," Chris agreed. "I'm on my way."

"I have been instructed by the Lord to get ready for a battle tonight, and you are to accompany me."

"That's fine. Where are we going?"

"We have to go to Summerset Boulevard and wait outside."

"What are we looking for?" Chris asked. "What can we expect to find there?"

"I have no idea, but whatever we find, we need to get ready for battle."

Battle? "Lord, I am the only one left without my name," prayed Chris, "but I am willing to fight. Thy will be done."

~*~

Beth Cooper and Reverend Milton relaxed in a luxurious room in the grand hotel on Summerset Boulevard.

Reverend Milton reached across the satin sheets and touched Beth's shoulder. "This should be a great night."

"It would be better if I could let everyone know you belong to me," Beth said as she turned and snuggled into him.

He ran his finger along her cheek. "You really pleased me this afternoon, Sweets. We will soon have a formal relationship, but we still need to wait a little bit longer."

"Okay, Honey," Beth sighed. "You know I love you."

Someone knocked at the door.

"That must be room service," Beth said. "I will take care of it. Go on to the shower, I will be right in with you."

"Okay, Babe."

A bellboy delivered Champaign in a bucket of ice, along with her favorite chocolates and a beautiful arrangement of flowers. She smiled. Robert must love her after all.

"Thanks," she said as she tipped the bellboy generously.

Beth arranged the gifts on the dresser top and admired them for a few moments before she stripped. She was going to bless Robert with a massage in the shower like he'd never received before.

The time passed quickly, and it was soon time for the couple to leave for church.

"I don't want to be without you for even one second," Beth said. "I don't want to go drive church alone."

"But, Sweets you have your own car."

"I know. You haven't even left, and I miss you already."

They got dressed, and Robert walked Beth to her car. He put his arms around her and gave her the best kiss ever. Surely he was telling her the truth about his love.

~*~

Sandra and Chris watched Reverend Milton escort Beth out of the hotel.

Chris stiffened. "What is he up to?"

"I'm surprised to see him here," Sandra said. "I expected to see him at church tonight."

"There is still time, maybe he's on his way there now," Chris said.

Reverend Milton opened Beth's car door and tenderly helped her inside, then strolled two spaces over and climbed into his own.

Chris started his engine and he and Sandra followed the two cars heading toward the church.

When they parked at the church, Chris noticed Reverend Milton's car was empty. A dark cloud hovered over Beth's car, and she was still inside.

Chris got out and approached her. "Hi, Beth, you've been busy today, haven't you?"

Her eyes widened. "I don't understand what you mean."

"How long have you been dating Reverend

Milton?"

At the question, Beth slapped Chris, leaving a red mark on his face.

Sandra rushed to his side.

"Get ready for battle," the Elite Commander said.

Chris saw Psychic was ready for battle, and felt his own armor descend upon him. His new name, *Marvel,* was written on his right shoulder.

Succumbus came out of the cloud hovering over Beth's car and morphed into a big spinning tornado.

The tornado aimed toward *Marvel* and *Psychic.*

No one was in the parking lot except for three individuals. All the other cars were empty.

Suddenly the big tornado dipped and lifted Marvel into the air, throwing him to the far end of the lot.

Psychic managed to swing her weapon, a short, slightly curved Cutlass saber with a basket-shaped guard. She sliced through the tornado.

The tornado morphed into a large four headed wolf. The wolf yipped and bared its teeth to bite Psychic.

Marvel ran from the edge of the lot where Succumbus had thrown him, and came to Psychic's rescue.

One swing of Marvel's 40 inch long curved Swiss Sabre cut off one of the wolf's heads.

With another swing, Psychic cut the second head. The two remaining heads snapped sharp white teeth at them.

Succumbus managed to knock Psychic and Marvel to the ground, and prepared to attack their heads.

Psychic's Cutlass saber merged with Marvel's Swiss Sabre, creating a long, broad flying axe with a two-edged blade fastened on a lengthy pole with a silver chain attached. With directions from the Elite Commander, the two-man-team was able to whirl this new combined weapon from a distance so they could slash their weapon in close contact with the enemy.

"Throw and pull," the Elite Commander said.

Together they threw the long, broad flying axe into the air.

The new weapon appeared as a huge constellation in a swirling motion and in varying heights, coming toward the opponent.

"You missed," Succumbus said as the axe flew past. "It is my turn now,"

The two-man-team pulled back on the chain, and the flying axe returned with a tremendous power cutting off Succumbus' two remaining heads, which rolled across the parking lot.

Marvel and Psychic were not severely injured,

but the victory was worthy.

However Beth Cooper lay unconscious on the ground.

Some of the cars had broken windows, and the cost of the damage remained to be seen.

As their armor disappeared the warriors carried Beth into the church and laid her on a padded bench in the foyer.

"Should we confront Reverend Milton now, or wait until the end of the service?" Chris asked.

"Do not engage. You are not yet ready for more," the Elite Commander said. "Wait for your training."

Chapter 18

On Thursday morning, the team members gathered at Michael's house.

Anthony once again took charge as leader. "Time for roll call. I will say your names and if you're not here, please speak up." He grinned as he called off their names.

Each one tried to outdo the others with a smart come back.

"Okay, that's it," Anthony continued as he checked off the last name. "Big Jax, Josh, and Daniel Samuels are waiting for us in Slattersville. Let's pray for guidance and protection before we head out."

He bowed his head. "Abba Father. Holy One. We come humbly before you, the only true God. We admit we are weak and can do nothing without you. Forgive our past arrogance in rushing ahead of your plans for us. Prepare us for this battle, which is yours. Amen."

"Do not fear, for I am with you," said the Elite Commander.

"Let's head out," Anthony said. "Daniels will meet us at the town entrance. He said it's far too dangerous for us to enter the town on our own after Koroshiya San's warning."

Forty-five minutes later the team made it to the entrance where they saw the old warrior waving his hands in welcome.

Michael opened the back door and slid over in the seat. "Jump in."

The Emissary grinned. "Don't mind if I do."

True to His word, at that moment the Elite Commander placed a protective shield over the team, and they were invisible to both human and demon's eyes.

As they drove through the town and toward the back road, the Emissary directed them to the mansion where Big Jax and Josh waited.

When they entered the property, the protective shield expanded like a cloud cover to envelope the mansion and grounds in full.

Anthony nodded in satisfaction. No one would see what was happening inside.

~*~

"My Prince, I detected some weird presence and power by the Emissary's house," Botis reported.

Apollyon puffed out his chest. "Go, check it out. Let me know what you discover."

"Absolutely," Botis said. "There is something going on with that old sluggard."

"He should have remained inactive. We cannot let anything upset our plans for this town." Apollyon frowned. "Be sure to keep me informed."

"Yes, My Prince." Botis bowed and stepped backward.

~*~

Beth was still unsure what had happened last night. Was it just a dream as Robert said? For her it was a nightmare.

But if it wasn't a dream, what then? Did I really see Chris and Sandra? Did they uncover my sin? Why can't I remember everything?

She couldn't stand it any longer and called Robert.

"You need to stop calling me every day, Beth. You know we have to lay low."

"What's wrong, Robert. Why are you so distant?" Beth burst into tears.

"What's this? Are you ok, Babe?"

"I tried to tell you last night. I really need to talk to you."

"Okay, just a moment."

Beth heard Robert's muffled voice telling someone he needed to take this call.

"I should have a few moments now."

"I'm scared, Robert. I can't get any of it out of my mind. I'm shaking and frightened to death."

"Just a moment I am going to a place that is more private."

When he gave her the go ahead, Beth recited

everything she could remember about her experience in the parking lot, but when she mentioned the swords and warriors, Robert interrupted.

"How much Champagne did you drink, Babe? Sounds like a hallucination but don't worry, at the very least, it was all a bad dream. You simply fell asleep at the church, nothing to worry about, Sweetheart."

Even with Robert's reassurance Beth didn't feel at ease. Should she have mentioned talking to Chris? Should she warn him Chris and Sandra might know about their affair?

~*~

Anthony followed Daniel to the front entrance of his large and beautiful home.

Daniel turned and raised his hands as in a benediction. "Welcome, my friends. We will be spending a lot of time here in my humble abode, as this is going to be our training facility."

"How is this going to work?" Anthony asked. "What is the plan?"

"Come in and get settled." Daniel opened the door and ushered the team inside.

"Hey, guys," Josh said, as he rose from the sofa.

Michael moved toward him with outstretched arms. "So good to see you on the outside and not surrounded by prison bars."

Anthony waited until the others were settled in and then found a place to sit beside his sister.

"As you already know," Daniel said. "I have several rooms here. Big Jax and Josh are already staying with me. Tadd is working nearby, so, I would like to extend the invitation for him and Chris to move in during our training as well."

Chris grinned and nodded. "Works for me."

"Thanks," Tadd said with a glance at Abby.

Anthony hadn't missed the way Tadd had made sure to sit near Abby. *It will do him good to not see her so often.* Not that Anthony disapproved of the growing romance between them. But he also didn't want them to be distracted in battle.

"I understand some of you cannot move here, because of your responsibilities in Clanston," the Emissary continued. "But you will still need to come here for training."

"Agreed," Anthony said. "I had a thought though. With your permission, before we start going over the agenda perhaps we should fill the Slattersville members of the team in on what went down in Clanston last night."

"By all means," Daniel said. "Give us a report."

Sandra began by telling them about her direction to go to Summerset Boulevard.

Then Chris explained the meeting between Robert Milton and Beth they had witnessed in the hotel parking lot the evening before.

Janet's complexion paled. "He's seeing Beth? I hadn't picked up on that at all."

Chris seemed to avoid looking her way. "I confronted Beth before the evening service at New Hope Trinity Church," he said. "At first, she denied everything, and then when I told her what we had seen, she slapped me."

"Evil spirits tore through the church parking lot that night and broke a lot of the car windows," Sandra said.

"We saw the dark shapes inside Trinity Church, and expected to suit up for battle."

"But the Elite Commander told us to wait, that we were not ready for this fight."

"And here we are, eager for training," Chris finished.

Chapter 19

Anthony waited until the rest of the team had settled in and then found a seat in Daniel's massive living room.

"Welcome to your first training." Daniel looked around the room, including all of them in his glance. "I've been praying and hoping to fulfill the tasks which our Lord has entrusted to me."

Daniel nodded to Anthony. "Also you will all be called by your new names during the training. Therefore, I will need each one of you to state your warrior name, starting with the leader."

"My name is *Warrior*," Anthony said.

"And I'm *Faith Woman*," said Janet.

Michael nodded. "*Shrewder*."

"I am called *Polyglot*," Josh said.

"*Decipher*." Big Jax's deep voice rolled across the room.

"*Psychic*," Sandra said with a nod.

Erin pointed to herself. "I'm *Mender*."

"*Marvel*." Chris gave a tilt of his head.

"I am the *Discerner*, "Abby said.

And I'm the *Judge*, "Tadd said with a grin.

"Thank you very much. We will get into the meaning of your names a bit later. As you all know, my name is the *Emissary* and for an introduction I will tell you my story."

Anthony relaxed back into his seat, waiting to hear how God had trained Daniel, or as they were to call him, the Emissary."

"Many years ago the Lord put a very wise man in my path. A dear and beloved elder named, Watsuki Gensai. As his name indicates, he was Japanese. The man was tall and very strong, but with a heart of a child. And thanks to his training and teaching, I stand before you today with specific instructions and experience to share." He looked at each one of them and didn't move his eyes to the next person until he received a nod of recognition.

"Today, we will have a general introduction to what we will be learning. For those not staying here, I would like you to commit to a full day here every other Sunday. And perhaps another day or two through the week. Can you do that?"

Anthony looked at the others from Clanston. They nodded. "Yes, we can," he said. "How many weeks do you expect our training to take?"

"It will all depend on your understanding, skills and given gifts as well as the goal the Lord wants for each one of you."

"Yeah, but can you give us an approximate

time?"

"My training took me six months. Since those who progress quicker will help the others, God willing, I expect to complete yours in half of that time."

The Emissary nodded toward Big Jax. "And of course those staying in my shack will be training on a daily basis."

"We will try to meet your expectations," Big Jax said.

"Here is your first rule. Do not engage in any battle with the enemy during your training." Again the Emissary looked at each one of them. "I can't stress this too much. You are not allowed to engage in any battle at all."

"But what if we face a situation where we have no choice?" Michael asked. "What about those times we *have* to fight?"

"You will need to avoid those types of situations. Plus, the Elite Commander has provided a protective shield for each of you. You will be invisible to the eyes of the enemy during your training."

"Heavy," Michael said.

"We'll start by teaming you up into five pairs."

"Do I get to pick my partner?" Josh asked as he glanced at the others.

"Unfortunately, no. The Elite Commander has given me specific instructions for the pairing.

Team one will consist of *Warrior and Mender.*"

Erin moved closer to Anthony.

"Team two will be *Shrewder and Faith Woman.*"

With a nod, Janet walked toward Michael.

"Team three is *Decipher and Polyglot.*"

Big Jax and Josh were already sitting close and Big Jax punched or rather bumped Josh's shoulder.

"Team four is *Psychic and Marvel.*"

"Great. We've already been working together," Sandra said as she glanced at Chris.

"And Team five is the *Judge and Discerner.*"

Tadd grinned.

"You've each been given specific gifts from the Spirit. Some have been given more. But each of you excels in at least one very specific gift, which you will learn to use mightily throughout this training."

"Thank you for that," Anthony said. He didn't want to lead this team into a trap ever again.

"I need all of you to stand in battle position with your hero's transformation."

"We cannot transform ourselves," Anthony protested. "Whenever there is a battle to fight our hero's transformation occurs automatically."

"That's about to change. You need to learn how to control the transformation. This is going to be our first task."

"But how?"

"When you saw me for the first time, I was wearing my warrior transformation, and when you picked me up today I was also wearing my warrior transformation, wasn't I?" Right at that moment, the *Emissary* transformed in front of their eyes. "As you can see, there is no battle to fight."

"How did you do that?" Chris asked.

"The key for controlling your transformation is very simple, but at the same time, very powerful. You must believe in the gift of transformation with your whole mind, body, soul, and spirit to be able to control it."

"Heavy," Michael said.

"Pay close attention. Prayer is the key. It is a constant reminder of who is transforming you. "In the name of the Father, the Son and the Holy Spirit, transform."

Daniel Samuels stood before them in full armor, bequeathed with the name EMISSARY, engraved on his right shoulder.

"Where did the gemstones come from?" Janet asked. "I didn't see them before."

The Emissary's brass armor gleamed lavender from his helmet, breastplate, and belt to his shield. Poudretteite gemstones filled his armor, and as he moved his whole image glittered like a multi colored rainbow. His lavender Spartan's sandals flaming fire as he pranced before them.

"Each of you will also have new armor," the Emissary said. "Your weapons will each be unique to you and used for a specific purpose." He raised the sword in front of his chest and rested the blade in the palm of his armored left hand. "Mine is a Silver Knights of Heaven Sword named 'Heavenly Rain.'

"Now see if you can transform."

"In the name of the Father, the Son, and the Holy Spirit, transform," the team said in unison.

"Very good. Now when you want or need to resume your normal form you just say your name "*Emissary off.*"

The team turned their transformation off and waited for the Emissary's next order.

"You may be seated." The Emissary waited until they were all settled.

He nodded approval. "Each of you will come up here one at a time beginning with Warrior, and we will observe the transformation."

Daniels stepped back with the others and Anthony took his place.

"In the name of the Father, the Son and the Holy Spirit, transform."

Anthony's new armor, with the name WARRIOR engraved on his right shoulder glowed black gold and was filled with garnet gemstones that flashed red and then blue like a billion stars. And his black Spartan's sandals also flamed fire as he ambled a bit.

"Walk like a warrior and hold up your sword," the Emissary said.

Anthony grinned and pranced before them raising his new sword with a wide curved steel blade.

"Warrior carries a Mameluke crossed hilted sword," the Emissary said.

"That is so incredible," Janet said. "Warrior really looks like a warrior, doesn't he?"

"Okay, Mender," the Emissary said.

Anthony and Erin switched places.

"In the name of the Father, the Son and the Holy Spirit, transform."

Erin stood proudly in her new jewel studded armor with MENDER, engraved on her right shoulder. She held up her weapon and pranced allowing the others to see her Spartan's sandals flaming fire just as Anthony's had done.

"Mender's Espada Ropera sword, is of Spanish origin. It is light-weight with a thin blade. As you can see it's an unusually ornate dress sword," the Emissary said.

Anthony shrugged. "Guess I can cover for you."

"Don't be fooled by the sweet look of her weapon," the Emissary said. "Time for Shrewder to show his stuff."

Erin and Michael switched places.

"In the name of the Father, the Son and the Holy Spirit, transform."

With SHREWDER engraved on his right shoulder, Michael's new armor glowed golden red from the many Painite gemstones, resembling the flame of a thousand fires. The glow concealed his sword. He marched around a bit as the others did and his red Spartan's sandals flamed fire.

"As you can see, although Anthony and Erin's jeweled armor matched, the Shrewder's is different. In fact each team will have matching armor, but each warrior will have different weapons. Hold up your sword," the Emissary directed.

Michael pranced up and down before them holding up his sword.

"The Shrewder carries, an Aikuchi Katana. This weapon has a hand-forged tempered blade. When we begin the fight you will see what his weapon can do."

The Emissary nodded to Janet. "Faith Woman."

Janet took Michael's spot in the limelight.

"In the name of the Father, the Son and the Holy Spirit, transform."

With FAITH WOMAN on her right shoulder. And with the addition of a red cape, Janet strutted her stuff. Her cape swirled and her Spartan's sandals flamed fire as she stalked across the floor holding her straight, single edged sword. She looked from left to right as if prepared for battle.

"Faith Woman carries a Japanese Chokuto Sword. It is made for cutting and thrusting," the Emissary announced.

"Ouch," Big Jax said. "That brings back memories. I'm glad I'm on your side now."

"Decipher, you are next."

Big Jax was a big man. But a humbled man. His body shielded away from the limelight even as he moved forward.

"Be strong and courageous. The Lord is with you." the Decipher said. "In the name of the Father, the Son and the Holy Spirit, transform."

Carrying the name of DECIPHER on his right shoulder, Big Jax's new armor radiated blue. His Blue golden helmet, blue diamond shield, blue bronze breastplate, and blue silver belt are filled with Musgravite gemstones flashing dark violet and grayish light. His blue Spartan's sandals flamed fire as he walked before the rest of the team.

"As you can see the gemstones sparkle along Decipher's armor like a billion individual stars. This is an advantage which makes him invisible in the shadows until his opposition is within his reach."

Big Jax stood tall as the Emissary spoke. He appeared fearless and able to be brutal in a blink of an eye.

"Our Decipher needs weapons to match his size and character. He carries a Kodachi sword, a combination of a ninja and samurai sword and a companion sword of normal size. The second sword has a hidden handle," the Emissary said.

Anthony shifted in his seat. *I'd hate to meet him in a dark alley at midnight.*

"Polyglot," the Emissary said.

Josh advanced to the front. "I'm glad Decipher is on my team," he said. "In the name of the Father, the Son and the Holy Spirit, transform."

In the blink of an eye Josh was fully armored, with POLYGLOT engraved on his right shoulder.

His legs visibly twitched and fire shot from his Spartan's sandals. "It's almost like the armor is controlling me."

"It's okay. We need to show off a bit today. You will learn control with training," the Emissary explained. "Polyglot's weapon is a 24-inch blade Messer sword or 'great knife.' The blade is single-edged with a cross-guard protrusion at the side which protects his hands."

"Does the Lord choose which weapons we will use?" Sandra asked.

"That's right Psychic, and it's your go." The

Emissary nodded to her.

"In the name of the Father, the Son and the Holy Spirit, transform."

Her new armor glowed like the midday sun. Her name, PSYCHIC, on her right shoulder seemed to pulsate. Sandra was swathed in a golden-pink helmet, and a pink diamond shield. Even her bronze breastplate had a pink tint. Deep blue and yellow Jeremejevite gemstones decorated her armor. Her pink Spartan's sandals looked delicate and feminine but even they flamed fire as she kicked up her heels and held up her weapon.

"As you can see Psychic carries a short, broad Cutlass saber that is slightly curved with a basket-shaped guard," the Decipher said. "Don't be fooled by her dainty look. It is for the benefit of the enemy."

"I wondered what the Lord was thinking," Chris said. "I am going to need her backup."

"And you will have it." The Emissary nodded to Chris.

"In the name of the Father, the Son and the Holy Spirit, transform?"

"Once more, son. This time with confidence."

Chris filled his lungs and his chest puffed out. "In the name of the Father, the Son and the Holy Spirit, transform."

Immediately Chris was bathed in a glowing

haze. MARVEL was engraved on his right shoulder.

"Marvel wields a Swiss Sabre sword with a 40-inch blade. As you can see it is slightly curved resembling the beak of a bird."

"Oh, my. It does," Janet said.

"The hilt of his sword is exquisitely formed with a pommel that is a trefoil shape, like a stylized clover in which a single-looped bar forms the back-guard," the Emissary continued as if he had not been interrupted by Janet's exuberance.

"The different weapons the Lord has provided each of us is amazing," Chris said. "I only hope I can learn to use this."

"The Spirit has not made a mistake in the weapons He chose. You will see when we get into the weapon training. Tadd, you're next."

"In the name of the Father, the Son and the Holy Spirit, transform."

The transformed Tadd radiated golden-purple. And as expected, JUDGE was engraved on his right shoulder. His golden helmet had a purple aura, his shield a glittering purple diamond, and all his armor was decorated with red beryl gemstones encircled with streams of gold bands, reflecting the brilliant colors of deep aquamarine and emerald. His purple Spartan's sandals flamed fire as he held up his weapon and pranced before the others.

"The Judge wears a Dao sword of forged steel with a single, wide blade. As you see it is moderately curved and boasts a hilt with a disc-shape cup." The Emissary nodded toward Abby. "Last but not least."

"In the name of the Father, the Son and the Holy Spirit, transform."

The DISCERNER stood gloriously before them.

"Our Discerner wields a Swiss Katzbalger side-arm Sword," the Emissary said. "Your final lesson for today is very important. In a team battle, your partner is your back eyes and shield. The battle formation is back to back."

The pairs found each other and stood back to back, glancing at their instructor for approval.

"Remember, you and your partner are one in a battle. If you manage to fight as one, you will be undefeated."

The training continued during the day, practicing transformation and battle formation for each team. It took some time for the team to manage the transformation perfectly each time, because they needed to believe the key-phrase for transformation, as well as say it. By the end of the day they had each mastered their first training session.

"You've done a great job today, I am

impressed." The Emissary beamed at the group. "If we continue like this, we might finish quicker than I projected."

Chapter 20

Sunshine filtered through the stained glass windows filling the sanctuary of New Hope Trinity with light. No dark shadows or clouds appeared anywhere in the large room.

With a lilt to her step Janet left the other team members in the pew and walked toward the organ.

As she passed Beth Cooper and Nina Patel. They smiled and whispered to each other in a peaceful scene. Janet continued past the bench where Reverend Robert sat beside Rick Watson and took her place at the organ.

Reverend Robert smiled her way. Was that a hint of longing in his eyes? So was he still available? Had it all been an illusion that he was seeing Beth?

Janet lifted her hands and plunged them to the organ's keys as she began a resounding hymn by Isaac Watts.

~*~

News came from the prison that Big Jax the dragon had been released.

"What?" Sammie asked "How is that possible? Where is he?"

"I want everyone to start the search and look for that traitor," Viper said. "He and his so-called partner will pay for what they have done."

"There is no trace of him," Williams said. "I have been trying to trace the Boss, but—"

"He ain't no boss nomore," Viper interrupted with a huff. "Watch your tongue!"

"I will use all my influence to track him down," Koroshiya San said. And when I find him, we will surely get the answers."

"Put him out of his misery, you mean," Viper said.

"Business is better than ever and we have full control of Slattersville," said Koroshiya San. "We might need to think on locating another ghost town soon."

Viper slapped Koroshiya San on the back. "Sounds like a great idea, but we will need to consult with *The Lord of the Night.*"

The others trembled at the mention of this name.

"Let us continue our operations here," Viper said. "I am sure he will contact us shortly after receiving our latest report."

~*~

Botis stood before Apollyon with head bowed. "My Prince, there seems to be a very powerful presence and a large concentration of light coming from the shack of the old sluggard, the one called the *Emissary."*

The dark prince nodded. "Yes, I have sensed it too, something is going on over there, but somehow it's always overcast, and I cannot see what is happening. Didn't I send you to check on it?"

"It appears to be a thick cloud covering but when I flew down to penetrate I bounced as it I had hit a shield of armor, my Prince."

"Let's reinforce our squad and be ready for anything. We have pending business with this so called team. I still do not know all the members, but you have been doing a great job."

"Thank you My Prince," said Botis with a bow.

"It is time for my general commanders to be given specific tasks and beef up our human creations."

"Yes, My Prince, at your service."

"Mastema stay with Viper Chambers *"the Snake."*

Mastema, smacked the lips of both his crowned heads with delight.

"Malphas," Apollyon continued. "Go with Koroshiya San *"the Assassin."*

The stealthy wolf, second in command under Satan, growled appreciatively.

"Samael stay with Pat Williams "the Python".

Presenting as a black "king" snake, Samael flashed his green eyes and his long divided tongue flickered.

"Botis go with Sammuel Strong *"Sammie."*

"Yes, My Prince."

Legion stay with Kimura Ichi *"Evil Sword."*

Sometimes called Breath of Satan, Legion's huge glistening eyes filled with pride. She twirled and her glorious crown framed by a headdress of feathers and strands of hair swirled with the spinning action. "Yes, My Prince," she proclaimed in a high velocity voice.

"I will stay with *The Lord of the Night*, the Boss of Bosses, whose name is yet forbidden to speak. Remember, confuse, deceive, cheat and destroy. Take your evil squads with you all."

"Yes, My Prince. Yes, My Prince," answered the five evil commanders as they departed with thousands of evil slaves.

~*~

"Becky and I planned this while the rest of you were in Slattersville," Deborah told the team as they filed to the large dining room table.

Becky set a platter of food on the table. "You do too much, Deborah. It was time I chipped in and helped."

"And what a treat to be able to share with you here in the privacy of our home," Michael said. "Especially since we won't all be here next week."

Deborah straightened and looked at her husband. "Whatever do you mean?"

"Daniel wants me to stay with him during the training," Tadd said.

Chris nodded. "And he asked me to stay there as well."

"You're leaving us, Chris?" Deborah asked with a frown.

"Just for now," Chris said. "And I'll be back at least every other Sunday to take care of the children's ministry."

"When do the rest of you go back?"

"After today some of us will go every Sunday," Anthony said. "And we will schedule time to spend a full week as often as we can. Meanwhile we practice here at home."

"Will you show us what you learned?" Ben asked. "Please? Please?"

Anthony ruffled Ben's hair. "How about if we finish our meal?"

The others laughed.

"Dad, can Mom and I go with you next time?" Ben asked. "I want to see your sword and your armor. Please, Dad? Please?"

"What do you think, Michael?" Anthony looked toward their host. "We're all planning to go back tomorrow. Think we should take our wives so they can meet the other team members?"

"And, of course, we can repeat this splendid and yummy meal." Michael agreed.

"Sure thing," Deborah said with a nod from Becky.

"I am glad I will be at the mansion during the whole training, at least on my off hours from work," Tadd said, as he flexed and un-flexed his hands. "When I see all the demons and enslavers in the prison, I am eager to clean that place up." He stood and moved to a corner of the room. "In the name of the Father, the Son and the Holy Spirit, transform."

"Yay!" Ben yelled. "I see a Hero."

"Judge off".

Ben's countenance fell as Tadd resumed his normal look. "Do it again!"

~*~

Back at the Markson's new apartment, Anthony found a private spot to practice. "In the name of the Father, the Son and the Holy Spirit, transform."

At one of his transformations, Ben caught him.

"Warrior off."

"Awesome Dad." Ben jumped up and down and clapped his hands. He looked around. "Is there a demon around? Are you going to fight now?"

"Hey, Buddy. I am just practicing. You know Daddy needs to train."

"Sure, Dad. Can I see it again?"

And once again Anthony transformed.

"That is so cool, Dad. I want to be a warrior too."

"Patience, Son. When the time is right, you will be."

Chapter 21

This time, the team didn't need to watch for the *Emissary* at the entrance to Slattersville. By now they realized the shield of invisibility would take them through the town unnoticed.

They continued on their way and soon passed the security gate to the mansion and headed toward the residence.

"We're here," Anthony said as he pulled to a stop. "Everybody ready?"

"Deborah, you will absolutely love the kitchen," Abby said.

Before they had even reached the door of the mansion, Daniel walked onto the porch.

"Welcome," their instructor said. "Who are these two beautiful women?" He bent down to Ben's level. "And who is this fearsome young warrior you've added to the team?"

Anthony chuckled. "This is my wife, Becky and my son, Ben Markson. I hope you don't mind that they came along."

"Not at all." Daniel looked at Becky. "It is very nice meeting you."

Ben pulled on the back of Anthony's shirt. "Hey, Dad. He called me a warrior."

Anthony grinned and the other adults chuckled. Ben was going to be a real character today.

Michael held his hand at Deborah's back. "And this is my lovely wife, Deborah. While we are training, these ladies would like to prepare us a very delightful meal."

"I hope you don't mind if we mess around in your kitchen," Deborah said.

Daniel beamed. "Not at all. Come in. Your addition to the day will be a blessing."

"Come along, Ben," Becky said. The ladies took the boy with them and went into the house.

The Emissary didn't move off the porch, indicating the team should stay outside for their training. "I am quite confident that you've all mastered flipping your transformation on and off. The question for today is, how do you spot the weakness of your opponent?"

As their instructor glanced at each one, they all gave a vague response. That is, until he came to the former soldier of the team.

"You analyze the enemy's movements and learn how to predict them," *Shrewder* said.

"Well said, being an expert in battle I would expect such an answer from you."

The Emissary continued. "You do not win a battle by the number of strikes, but by the effectiveness of one single strike."

"Do you really think we will ever win a battle with the demons with one blow?" Anthony asked. "Most of our fights have been spur-of-the-moment. And, with an opponent we have never faced before."

"I didn't say you would win by the first blow." the Emissary chuckled. "You win with the last blow."

Anthony's face twitched. He shouldn't be so quick to speak and sound like a fool.

"Sometimes it will seem as if your adversary has no weak or blind spots. But everyone has at least one. You just need to observe your opponent's movements until you finally see it."

"So what's to keep them from slicing us apart while we search for weak spots?" Chris asked.

"Granted, while you are searching for a weak spot, you cannot fight with all your strength," Michael said. "Your primary duty will be to protect yourself, avoid the hits of your opponent, and of course, sometimes throw a swing or two, to show your adversary that you are serious."

Daniel nodded. "When you discover the enemy's weak spot, go for it with all your strength. Do not be mistaken, in the battles to come it is game over if you are overcome by your enemy."

Chris shuddered.

"We will have preliminary training battles for

each pair today," the Emissary said. "Today, you will each discover your partner's weakness."

Anthony nodded. It was time.

"Team one, *Warrior* and *Mender,* suit up for battle."

"In the name of the Father, the Son and the Holy Spirit, transform."

Two fully clad warriors stood before the Emissary ready for battle.

"The rules for battle are simple. Discover the weakness of your opponent and strike."

Anthony nodded.

"Do not fear, in case of severe injuries, help is here." Daniel gestured toward *Mender.*

"Yikes," Erin said. "And I'm in the first squirmish. How am I to lay hands on myself if he whacks my head off?"

"I don't expect you to try to kill each other. I was talking about the likely hood of a nick or two. And, Mender, I do have a first-aid kit here if that makes you feel better."

No sooner had Daniel finished speaking than the clanging of swords filled the air.

"What's up, *Mender? A*re you afraid?" *Warrior* taunted,

"Not likely."

"You are really a strong opponent, *Mender,* who could have imagined." *Warrior* swung his sword in what he hoped was a surprise move, attempting to knock *Mender's* weapon out of her hand.

"You are not bad at all, *Warrior.* I must say, I am impressed. But it is time to finish this duel," *Mender* said as she lunged forward.

Warrior felt the hit to his left leg. "Not bad, but you missed your best shot." W*arrior's* sword gently touched *Mender's* neck. "Battle is over."

The day continued with more battles and some minor healing work by the *Mender.*

After the last duel the *Emissary* spoke. "I can see who our strongest warriors are and where I need to work with each of you. You have been rated today according to your strength level, and given a rank number. Any warrior with a rank number higher than ten is not ready for battle. Number ten is very strong. But to go lower, say eleven, well I am sorry but that's just not enough power to fight the evil we will face."

The team began to murmur between themselves. Daniel held up his hand for silence.

"Notice the rank number displayed on the right side of your chest. I'll throw you out a challenge. Perhaps we can see it strengthen during future fights."

Anthony gazed at the numbers displayed on the team's armor. *Polyglot* ten. *Discerner* nine. *Mender* eight *Faith Woman seven Marvel* six. *Judge* five *Psychic* four. *Decipher three.*

Shrewder two. Looks like all the others were up to battle. He glanced down at his own chest with a frown and then relaxed when he saw the number one. "Hey, all the ranks are covered," he said. "And we've all passed the strength test."

"The highest ranking warrior will take the lead in each pair. That might give some of you a challenge to surpass your partner," the Emissary continued.

Anthony winked at Mender as if to taunt her to try it.

"In the battlefield, you need to be sharp and measure the strength of your adversary. Whenever it's possible, don't engage in a battle with a stronger adversary than you are," the Emissary continued.

"Use caution because, some warriors have the ability to suppress their strength and keep it low. Sometimes, they don't want to be considered the strongest, even when they are. It can be a good war strategy."

Michael nodded. "That's right. If your opponent is overconfident they will make mistakes."

"With experience and practice you will also learn how to control your power level reading and how to hide it from your adversary. Then you can have an advantage by being able to decide when you want to show your real strength or a lower one."

The Emissary glanced at each one on the team and then continued. "Of course you cannot pretend to have a higher level. At least you cannot display a higher level of strength than what you really have."

He smiled then. "Okay, that's it. Let's go inside and see what delights await us."

The team headed for the house and the anticipated meal prepared by Deborah and Becky.

Smells from the kitchen permeated the foyer.

"Yummy," Big Jax said "Thank you gracious ladies."

"Do not forget me," Ben said.

Deborah laid her hand on Ben's head. "Yes. We couldn't have done this without the assistance of the great chef, Ben Markson."

Ben grinned from ear to ear, and the adults laughed.

"I saw you through the windows. It was awesome."

Anthony's eye's sought out Becky's. He hadn't thought. "Sorry."

Ben danced up and down. "Mom watched you too."

"What?"

"What can I say? We were dazzled by the armor and swords," Becky said. "But I doubt we would enjoy watching your battles with real enemies."

"After the meal you must share with each other the weakness you have discovered. In future days you will focus on strengthening your own weakness, and learn how to cover for your partner."

~*~

Meanwhile the evil squad was also growing in power and dominion. *The Lord of the Night* had a clear goal in his mind. His heart was to rule over Ohio as if it were his own small country.

He had set up his main operations in a strategic location in the very center of the state, taking all cardinal points of the unnamed town and controlling the only possible exits. In fact, he formed a compass strategic, which in the end would leave no room for exits or un-allowed entrance to the entire state.

It was time to send his followers a message. When the spirits assured him all were gathered in Slattersville, *The Lord of the Night* flipped on the speakers.

"I am very pleased with your outstanding performance," he said. "It is time for my top warriors to each lead his own operation and town."

He paused for a dramatic effect.

"*Snake*, you will continue in Slattersville and

become the ruler. This town is our North-West strategic point. We will spread out from there and surround the state with other sites of operation."

Viper Chambers, *Snake*, a lanky American with just enough French to cause his friends, as well as his enemies, to fear his penchant for exotic torture, has a power rank of five. He'd been with the evil one for so long he'd become closer to a reptile than an actual man.

His weapon of choice was a Joyeuse. The hilt of the sword with its heavily sculpted gold pommel was made in two halves with a long gold grip.

"Moving around the state we located a town in the South-West section of Ohio. Congratulations, *Python.* You will rule *Moonville.*"

The *Lord of the Night* was quite pleased with this exquisite beauty with a blackened heart. The Python had a power rank of four, earned by the atrocities of violence she had committed above and beyond that of any other warrior, male or female.

Her weapon of choice was a Tomoyuki Yamashita's Sword, a curved and forged blade of Japanese origin.

"*Assassin* you will take over and rule a new town named *Knockemstiff,* located in the Southern point of Ohio."

Koroshiya San, called the *Assassin* holds the power rank of one but *The Lord of the Night* may be the only one who knows it. The Assassin had always tried to conceal his true rank.

He carried a Honjo Masamune, blade of choice for the legendary priest and sword smith Masamune.

Valued as Japanese national treasures, they proved to be rare as only one other of these swords was ever found.

'Next we have *Sammie.* You will rule *Newville,* located in the East side of Ohio."

Strength and power not being quite the same thing, Sammuel Strong, *Sammie* with a power rank of three was considered to be as strong as any man that has ever lived. His ebony face was framed by long dread locks that hung to his shoulders. He carried a weapon dubbed 'The Seven-Branched Sword,' representative of his leadership of his tribe.

He was quite proud of the long iron sword with six branch-like protrusions along the central blade. The inscription found on the weapon was, 'This sword was made of one-hundred times hardened steel. The use of this sword has repelled one-hundred enemy soldiers.'

"*Evil Sword* you will rule *Blueball*, located in North-East Ohio."

An American with Japanese origin, Kimura

Ichi, Evil Sword held a warrior rank of two.

He sported a long braided beard of grey and white with his long straggly hair pulled back into a ponytail that reached his waist.

Kimura Ichi was a hunter of men in the worst sort of way. His weapon, the Kusanagi sword, isn't on public display and hasn't been seen except by this owner and swordsman. When not in use, it's always kept shrouded in wrappings. All those who have ever come in contact with this weapon have come upon disaster and death.

"I will disclose the center of the operation and my location when you five fierce leaders prove that you are worthy of ruling with me."

He waited a moment to let that soak in.

"You depart tonight. Get ready and prove that I was correct in my choice. Some of you already have your second in command and some have yet to choose one. However they will meet you at your respective towns."

The speakers clicked off.

It was the first time for some of the dark leaders to hear the actual voice of *"The Lord of the Night."*

They were honored and fearful at the same time.

~*~

Apollyon rubbed his hands together in glee as he considered battle formations and how to expand his dominion and enlarge his kingdom.

When *The Lord of the Night* finished lining up his human underlings, Apollyon addressed the spirit beings under his command.

"General orders have been issued, and you will rule along with my human followers at each new town. Guide them well, and use your incredible power to do what you know best."

"Yes, My Prince." The evil forces who had been assigned to these human puppets long ago, blasted off to the chant of, "Cheat, deceive, steal and destroy."

~*~

The *Emissary* sat on top of the building where he'd often watched the town in times past. He saw all the dark powers moving out of Slattersville. Some moved south and some moved east. A great darkness overpowered the road out of the town, but dark shadows still hovered over Slattersville.

Something big is on the move. Something huge is going down. "Lord, help us achieve our goal in time, because this darkness is spreading much too fast."

The Emissary flew down the big building unnoticed by anyone and retreated to his residence.

~*~

"I must select my second in command," said

Viper the *Snake*. "Listen up guys. Sammie is taking over another town. The position for my second in command is open. Those interested will fight for it, and the winner will prove worthy to be my right hand."

Three candidates offered to test their strength. Ross Wright, a very strong white man with dark eyes, also called *Shadow*, Payne Lestat, ex-marine force, with battle experience and expert in knives, also called *Blade*, and Synth Shade, a small but strong, black dude, also called *Muscles*.

"All right. Shadow and Blade have the first round."

With a smooth movement Blade managed to cut the throat of *Shadow* and that was the end of the fight. Blade had won easily and without much effort.

"You still up to the challenge, Muscles?"

When Muscles ambled over to Blade, Viper expected a fierce battle.

But *Blade* jumped on *Muscles* like a flying stone, and cut him in three tactic places.

Blade stood in front of *Muscles* with his hand raised in victory.

In the blink of an eye, Blade had hit Muscles in the sternum, temple, and right in the middle of his eyes.

"Impressive," said Viper.

Just as he was about to announce the name of his right hand, a voice from the crowd bellowed. "Hold it."

A handsome and slender man came forward. Raff Filtiarn, of Celtic decent, and whose last name means *Lord of Wolves.*

Viper recognized him as the silent one, always observing. He nodded. Nobody messed with this one. Just the look of his eyes made people not want to ask him anything.

The crowd yelled, "*owooooo, owooooo, owooooo.* Wolf. Wolf. Wolf!"

"You wanna die today, Wolf?" Blade asked. "So be it."

As *Wolf* approached, *Blade* jumped in the air.

With a single kick, Wolf knocked him to the ground.

Blade recovered, holding large sharp knives in both hands, "Your time is over, *Wolf.*"

In a heartbeat, *Wolf* managed to unarm *Blade.* Seconds later he killed him with his own knife— the Ulfberht.

His weapon of choice had one crucible steel blade with a geometric braid pattern, a double-edged blade, slightly curved marvel of 36 inches.

Blade fell onto his knees and his head hit the ground.

Wolf used his Ulfberht sword and cut off the head of his adversary.

"Is there no one else?" *Wolf* yelled. "Is there no one else?"

And Slattersville had its second in command.

Amaros was proud of his boy, he had wisely selected *Wolf.*

The demon *Amaros, the Watcher Angel—the Cursed One*—dressed in hunter's gear including a cap with folded-down flaps covering the eyes scattered over the back of his head—eyes that watched his victim.

Chapter 22

Things were going according to plan in the dark world. The evil ones were happily spreading their nets and their influence was growing.

The five evil-spirit commanders assigned an evil-spirit general to his second-in-command human puppet.

Mastema had assigned *Amaros* to whoever became second-in-command to Viper who now ruled Slattersville.

Amaros made sure Raff Filtiarn, the *Wolf,* became the *Snake*'s second-in-command.

~*~

Malphas had assigned Eligos to Garnet Dukes, who was called *Poisson Dagger.*

In human form, Eligos was 6 feet tall, with wavy blonde hair and deep blue eyes. Eligos ruled sixty legions of demons and reports only to the highest of officials. He was proud to be assigned to *Poisson Dagger.*

~*~

On the way to the town where Koroshiya San was the new ruler, his driver shared a story about the ghost town and how the name came into being.

According to the legend a preacher came across two women fighting over some dude. After hearing their story he advised the women that the man was not likely to be worth their trouble.

"In fact," the preacher said. "You would both be better off if someone should simply knock him stiff."

"But there ain't no church no more," the driver said, as he laughed at his own joke. "No sir, not even a hymn book left in this town."

Koroshiya San paid scant attention to the tale. The *Assassin* was eager to see his domain. This must be a very important location for *The Lord of the Night* to send him here.

Exactly an hour and forty-five minutes later, the driver delivered the *Assassin* to the entrance of the town, where Garnet Dukes, better known as *Poisson Dagger,* waited for him.

The *Assassin* had done his research. Garnet Dukes, with a power rank of seven, was of Spanish decent. However as a plus, he was raised in Japan under Samurai teaching.

After he'd entered the states, Dukes established his legacy as a ruthless and cruel individual. His weapon of choice was called 'burning stick' or 'firebrand.'

Poisson Dagger used fire to mark those he owned by way of degrading and defeating them.

"Welcome My Lord," *Poisson Dagger* said. "I have heard a lot about you. It is an honor to serve under your command."

"The driver was telling me how a once peaceful and happy little town like this came to be named Knockemstiff," the *Assassin* said. "Now he will give us a tour of the town."

After *Poisson Dagger* climbed into the back of the car beside the *Assassin*, their driver continued down the dusty road past several old dilapidated buildings, leaning on their foundations.

"There's only one local store on the unpaved main street of this town," the driver said. "They used to have a church."

He barked out a laugh. "Once the holy rollers left, very few decent people still live in this town. It seems like moonshiners are the main inhabitants."

The *Assassin* smiled. In a God-forsaken town like Knockemstiff, there were no boundaries to limit the demons from running wild through the country-side screaming for souls who might stumble into their territory.

And with Koroshiya San in charge, it was now the second most important town for evil human and spirit operations.

After the driver dropped them off at the building that would be their headquarters, the

Assassin and *Poisson Dagger* continued brainstorming the possible work load, inventory, town specifications, and areas for growth.

~*~

Samael had assigned *Asmodee* to Jack Mortas, commonly called *Panther.*

Asmodee, the most beautiful demon of all, typically presented as a graceful butterfly with every color of the rainbow in its wings.

However, the creature had presented as a gigantic moth with brilliant eyes and dull-brown wings extending from ceiling to floor the night Abby destroyed its influence on Tadd. As a moth Asmodee often wrapped its lustful wings around its victims in an attempt to smother.

Asmodee fluttered with pride around its puppet, the *Panther.*

~*~

The *Panther*, with a power rank of nine, had an IQ that would dazzle any professor. An American of Roman descent, he was able to think through any battle plan much like a master chessman.

And that evening, while he waited patiently for his boss, Pat Williams, the *Python* to arrive at Moonville, Jack Mortas solemnly and thoughtfully researched the town's history.

With the ability to see moves before they are made Panther read his opponent like a fine manuscript. He had at his beck and call some of the most brilliant leaders of the day, all ready to carry out the slightest command in the periphery of a play.

At a moment's notice, Panther's helpers slid in and out of the human chess game by a nod or a wink from him.

Nothing was more important to the Panther than accuracy and symmetry. That is why he preferred the Crocea Mors sword. Once wielded by Julius Caesar, the name of the weapon was Latin for 'yellow Death.'

According to Panther's research, railroad workers hated this area because it was the loneliest and most isolated eight miles they had to travel. In the end, even the rails were pulled up.

Once a very small mining town, all that remained of Moonville was a cemetery, a few foundations, and an abandoned railroad tunnel.

In the distant past plans had been made to restore the town of Moonville. But each time they were presented to a group of businessmen to pursue, the plans fell through.

The wind howled its lonely song through the abandoned town while rogue demon laughter was often heard in the dark nights.

After walking through the town, Panther nodded in appreciation. All would be well. In this town, evil had wide-open spaces to pursue its ugliest of deeds.

~*~

Botis had assigned Abdiel to Nash Sharpe, the *Black Scorpion*.

Abdiel was able to send his victims into a stinging nightmare. He considered himself multi-talented since he could morph into a woman, a man, or even a snake depending upon the best strategy for the kill.

As a woman Abdiel presented as a beautiful redhead with long hair, chained in the bonds of slavery.

As a snake Abdiel presented two python-shaped heads with fiery eyes.

As a man, Abdiel was a handsome, muscular being with a beautiful smile and deep blue eyes.

This demon used any sharp instrument—chains with razors, axes, swords, electrical wiring, even insects to focus on a particular nerve ending in the human body to execute the most torture, pain and ultimately death.

Abdiel looked forward to ruling this town along with his puppet, *Black Scorpion*.

~*~

Nash Sharpe, the Black Scorpion with an impressive rank of eight, received his name, not necessarily due to his race, but rather because he caused the deaths of his enemies by stinging.

Sharpe was a vicious executioner, whose nimble fingers and hands know the use of electrical impulses or sharp weapons to cause death.

He'd learned about the nerve locations in the human body from his father who was a doctor of sorts. He learned of pain and its sources from experiments practiced on his enemies.

For the Black Scorpion, the death of his enemies was, more often than not, made a matter of sport.

One of his most prominent weapons is the cherished Zulfigar, which refers to an Asian sword with two curved blades. This sword is a scimitar and a symbol of the Islamic faith.

At this moment Sharpe waited at the entrance of Newville town for his boss Sammuel Strong, *Sammie.*

Newville. The Black Scorpion shook his head in his mirth. There was nothing new about Newville.

The town once boasted powerful preaching and illustrious camp meetings. How easy it was, in the process of uncontrolled celebration, for evil to slip in amongst the worshipers.

Sharpe laughed out loud, because the unaddressed evil continued. And he was going to take pleasure at being in the center of it all.

Although the founders of Newville had great

plans, towns off the main path of the railway seldom survive. Newville was no exception.

A dam built on the Cuyahoga River would at times cause it to be flooded and after a few years of that the town was ordered abandoned.

Some foundations of the buildings were still standing in the forest just west of the lake. But Sharpe knew something still lived in Newville.

Evil survived when other things didn't, and evil had no opposition in Newville.

The Black Scorpion thrived, waiting for a weary soul to seek refuge here.

~*~

Legion had assigned Ipos to Iku Zai, *Flying swords.*

Ipos, the ultimate black cat, kept his victims cornered with his sharp and mesmerizing snow-white teeth. His emerald eyes observed all things, past, present and future. His head swung from side to side on his muscled body as he stalked his prey.

He beamed at his puppet Iku Zai knowing he had received the best choice of them all.

~*~

Iku Zai *Flying Swords* waited for Kimura Ichi, *Evil Sword* at the town of Blueball.

By looks, the slender blonde simply blended in with a thousand others. But her name stirred fear in the hearts of warriors everywhere.

American educated, her translated name meant violent evil and was descriptive of her very soul.

An expert swordswoman, with a power rank of six, she carried *The Cursed Muramasa*.

Her weapon was thought of as a demonic cursed blade that creates bloodlust in those who wield it.

The Muramasa brought tragedy, madness, and untimely deaths, both to the victims and the person who carried one.

Blueball, Ohio, a southwestern town of the state, had received its name because of an illiterate stage coach driver who could not read the sign, near the city limits, with the town's correct name on it.

To appease the irate citizens, the town council had erected a blue-colored metal sphere above the intersection of two roads at the heart of town. And once again, the stage coach stopped to pick up waiting passengers.

A large blue ball still hangs above the highway at the exit for Blueball. But no one remembered the original name of the ghost-town. Abandoned by most humans, something sinister had taken up residence there.

In the absence of law, lawlessness abounded. In the absence of peace and love, strife and hate thrived.

So it was, and so it would stay—in Blueball.

~*~

Word came for the first time of *Hell Town*, a very evil old town boasting a canal underneath the surface. Hell Town was the ideal place for *The Lord of the Night* and the main headquarters for all the operations for Apollyon.

Located in the center of Ohio, hidden in plain sight, only those who knew about Hell Town could find it.

Several cement buildings, a school, and a large garage housing old art displays and abandoned gas pumps stand, along with a visitor center that still served the few local visitors.

Rotted railway tracks meandered through the center of the town but the train had long left the station and so had the travelers. However train services were still active and available for their evil operations.

No visitors dared to take a day trip to Hell Town much less enter as the sun slipped down on this center of pure evil.

~*~

Each new town was able to service a wide area around it and was strategically situated approximately eighty miles from Hell Town.

Apollyon raised his arms in victory and spread his six leather wings as he surveyed his growing kingdom. Gratified to see how his dark influence was spreading throughout the state.

Chapter 23

Five months later the Emissary called the team together.

"You have worked hard and called on the hero within. These past few months have been grueling, but at the same time, very gratifying. You have come near to the end of your training, and you are worthy." He held up his index finger. "Yet there is one final lesson to learn."

He smiled and then continued. "Each of you has been given gifts from the Spirit honoring your names. Some of you have been given several gifts but there is one in particular where you will excel above all the others."

Daniel stood in front of Janet and took her hands. "*Faith Woman*, your special gift is easy to discern. It is the gift of faith. You are able to see what is not yet, as though it already was. You will bless many with your confidence in God's power."

He moved to Michael and laid hands on his shoulders. "Shrewder, the gift of wisdom will help you understand what to do in difficult situations. Stay close to God, for your wisdom is bound up in Him."

Daniel turned and reached for Abby's hands. "*Discerner*, to you has been given the gift of discernment. You can even discern between the spirits, whether they be of God. And you discern how to apply scripture in the circumstances you will find yourself in each day."

With one quick step Daniel stood before Josh and placed a hand on his back. "*Polyglot*, you have been given the gift of tongues. With this gift you have a type of discernment as well, for you will discern language."

When he reached Sandra, Daniel gently took her hands. "*Psychic*, you have been blessed with the gift of prophecy. You will bless many by teaching what you learn and know."

He smiled as he sidestepped and found Erin's hands. "*Mender*, you have already blessed us with the gift of healing. May you continue to do so."

Next, Daniel placed his hands on Chris's shoulders. "*Marvel*, the gift of miracles is not given lightly. God will use you to reveal Himself to others."

Daniel hesitated when he reached Big Jax. Then he placed his hands on the large man's biceps. "*Decipher*, you have been given the gift of interpretation of tongues. You will easily understand and learn language." He nodded. "No wonder our Lord paired you with Polyglot."

Daniel placed a hand on Tadd's back. *"Judge,* with the gift of knowledge you will have a special understanding of God and His ways. Listen for His voice and you will know when to speak and when to be silent."

As he stood before Anthony, Daniel put his hands on each side of the team leader's head. *"Warrior,* your gifts are very special. You've been given the gifts of revelation, power and inspiration. That is your burden for being the leader. You will excel in the one the situation requires of you the most."

He stepped back. "Congratulations, hero warriors. You are now ready for battle."

The team spontaneously threw up their hands. "Hurrah!" they cried "Hurrah!"

"While you've been training and gaining power, some of the evil forces have split off from Slattersville and moved on to other towns."

Michel shook his head in disgust. "We should have trained harder and faster."

The Emissary shook his head. "We can't get ahead of God's timing."

Anthony laid his hand on Michael's shoulder. "The rest of us learned that lesson the hard way, Michael. While you were still in prison we didn't wait. We went and checked out the town of Slattersville before the time was right. The Emissary is right. We cannot rush ahead of our

Lord." He shook his head. "Never again."

"Ohio has been trapped in a very dark and evil master plan, with evil forces controlling cardinal points of the state and closing possible exits or entrance to the towns that they control. I am aware of the most important five strike points of our enemy."

The team looked at their instructor expectantly.

"The Elite Commander has given each set of warriors a special assignment to implement together. Along with instructions for the training I have received specific tasks for each of the five pairs, and I have them here."

"Good to know," Anthony said.

"Each set of warriors will depart a week from now, on the same day and at the same time. You will leave our home base and strike the evil commanders by surprise and conquer those strategic towns that are currently controlling Ohio."

"We can do this." Anthony raised his fist and looked at the others on the team. "This time we know the Lord is sending us. This time we know the battle is His."

"That's right. Although your opponents are fearless and may be stronger than you, do not fear. The Lord has promised to be with you. Remember your training at all times and apply what you've learnt so you can make it through that day and come back conquerors. You will all strike the enemy on the same day."

"So should we meet somewhere in the center of the state on the day we are to leave?"

"No. This will remain our headquarters," the Emissary said. "As instructed by the Elite Commander I will hand an envelope to each pair with your new assignment. In the envelope you will find, the name of your target town, and the names of the leaders in the town, both humans and demons.

As the highest rank in each set opened the envelope, they read through the papers and then glanced at their instructor.

"I see the information in here, but what exactly is the assignment?" Anthony asked.

The Emissary beamed. "Good question. Please pay attention, because it goes for the assignment for each pair."

All eyes were on their instructor and no one spoke.

"You already know you have each been assigned to a town. Your task is to free the town from the oppression of the demons ruling it. Defeat the demons and their human puppets will be defeated as well."

"Let me at them," Big Jax said. "It is so good to be free of them and I want to deliver the others from their evil grasp as well."

"You need to kick out demon forces from these places, because the Elite Commander has plans for these ghost towns. Make no mistake. The battles are not going to be easy. Remember your training and trust in the Lord."

Daniel Samuels bowed his head. He was keenly aware of the great danger of the battles to come, but he was not allowed to share this information with anyone. And so it was.

~*~

Apollyon heard the news about the possible interventions to the towns. "I knew it was too good to last," he roared in anger. "Seems like the Lord should leave us alone. After all we only took over towns no one else wanted."

He immediately sent word to the leaders in each town to get ready and prepare for battle. The message had clear instructions. "Take no prisoners. Do not let anyone escape. Chop off the heads of the intruders and send them to me."

The evil teams were eager to taste blood.

The human evil commander known as *Lord of the Night—Boss of Bosses* never used his given name for the protection of both friend and foe. His weapon was more powerful than all of his teammates put together.

The Lord of the Night was graceful and dreadful all at the same time. He surpassed evil.

And for any who dared to look his way twice, he wielded his weapon like the trained Japanese samurai warrior that he was. And no one crossed his path.

Many attempted to rise in the ranks by getting close to him and learning his name but most didn't live to tell the tale. No, they simply disappeared into the night and others could only guess their fate. And no one challenged him.

The *Lord of the Night* sent words for each one of the dark human leaders.

"Get ready for battle. Some intruders are trying to take over our towns. Prove you are worthy, and do not spare anyone."

Every evil leader was ready for battle. They were born for this. They were born to kill, and they would gladly honor their towns by slaughtering the coward interlopers attempting to infiltrate their turf.

Although they had no idea who to expect or who they were looking for, the evil leaders did not worry or care. The result would be inevitable.

~*~

The hero warriors spent the week prior to the battle as a preparation week for the team, much like the Feast of Unleavened Bread before the Passover for the Israelites.

They focused themselves in assimilating all the details of their previous training, praying, worshiping, reading the Bible, and spending time with their families.

The night before the great battle, the team members agreed to have a meeting at Michael's house. It wasn't the center of Ohio, but they had decided to have all night devotions as a team.

Even Daniel Samuels agreed to leave Slattersville for the first time in many years. "The occasion is worthy," he said.

Michael and Deborah managed to find a large round table and seated all the team members by rank, starting from the lowest in rank up to the highest.

Of course Daniel was considered a guest. After all, Daniel was not going to fight. He was only the trainer for the team. And no one knew his strength, or rank number.

Around 10:00 pm Deborah retired and Janet turned over her bedroom to Becky and Ben.

The rest of the night passed with great anecdotes and stories shared between the team members, mingled with their prayers.

"And if you need to jump and leap, remember to keep your bottom away from your flaming sandals," Erin said with a giggle. "Cause it might be awhile before I can get to you and heal up the blisters."

After every lighthearted joke, another of the team members would offer up a serious prayer.

It was a very strengthening night for all the heroes because they knew they needed to be fortified against what they would face in a just a few hours.

~*~

Finally, morning came and it was time for each set of hero warriors to begin their journey to face the unexpected.

Each one of the five targeted towns were about the same distance from the center of Ohio. But, of course, the team members were in Clanston which was not in the center of Ohio at all, so the teams would not arrive at their target at the same time.

Anthony had rented five fast vehicles full of fuel to see them to their destinations and home again.

"Let the battles begin!" screamed *Apollyon* from an unknown location.

The team members looked at each other. They could not yet determine the location of this evil and terrifying laugh, but they all heard the words, and they got the message. They headed for their vehicles.

It was time.

Chapter 24

Anthony followed the directions carefully. With his foot on the accelerator he prayed for clear roads as the Mustang flew down the highway toward Knockemstiff.

Erin did a fine job of navigating and they soon turned onto a dusty road with a dilapidated sign pointing the way to the deadly ghost town that was their target.

"How sad that what used to be a peaceful and happy little town has become the place for one of our biggest battles to fight the forces of the darkness."

About a mile from the town Anthony hid the car in the trees. He and Erin transformed and walked to the town.

Warrior, with a number *one* on his right chest, represented a *Black Garnet Gemstone Knight*, carrying his Mameluke sword, especially used by Marine officers. His black Spartan's sandals flamed fire as he marched toward Knockemstiff.

When he and Mender were about one-hundred feet away from the town's entrance, Warrior spied his opponent and rushed to meet the giant of a Japanese American standing in front of the gate.

He was well matched with Koroshiya San who also displayed a rank of one on his left chest.

The Assassin met the attack boldly, with a mighty strike from his unique Honjo Masamune sword.

"Not so fast, shouldn't we get acquainted first?"

Warrior snorted and went for his second attack.

Both jumped so high it looked like they were flying. They met in the air hitting each other's blades.

Mender and Poisson Dagger stood in awe. The view was so incredible and the mighty strength coming out of each strike almost blew Mender and Poisson Dagger away.

But the battle was also playing havoc with of the buildings around them.

"At this rate we will destroy the town," Warrior said.

"Yes, indeed," Assassin responded. He pointed to the large mountain nearby. "Let us move up yonder for our battle."

They ran forward in combat position not losing each other's eyes for a single second. Both held fast to their mighty swords and shrieked out their own war cry.

~*~

Their husbands had been with the team preparing for this day and although Becky and Deborah were not fully aware of the dangers and complications that day might bring to them, they had decided to stay together.

They felt the tug of the Holy Spirit calling them for prayer and intercession.

Becky thought Ben was playing quietly in the other room, but the six-year-old boy jumped onto the couch. "Mom and Aunt Deborah, can we pray for Daddy and his team?"

When they heard the words coming out of the mouth of the young child, it did not sound like a suggestion at all, it came out more like a mandate and so it was.

They could not stop the spiritual force inside them praying for *The Warrior* and the Lord's team.

~*~

Mender and Poisson Dagger stood side by side as if they were friends, and watched the first in command fight in the sky.

When they were out of sight the medium height black warrior turned to Mender. "I am Garnet Dukes better known as Poisson Dagger." His rank of seven displayed on his arm. "I guess we can start our fight now. The boss is busy." He lifted his famous Tizona sword which is often called a burning stick or firebrand.

"I guess so. It looks like we are ready." Mender came out of the daze the blazing fight had put her in and touched her light weight, thin blade *Espada Ropera* Sword for courage although Poisson Dagger held a higher rank than the number eight displayed on her chest. "But it's not too late to switch sides, you know." She kicked her Spartan sandals and an impressive shot of fire flew behind her as she held up her weapon and shifted in a circle around Poisson Dagger.

"Now why would I want to do that?" Poisson Dagger seemed confident with the outcome of the battle, since he was stronger than Mender. "*¡Que comience la fiesta!*"

Mender shrugged. "You had your chance." She didn't even pay attention to his rank once the battle began.

~*~

Poisson Dagger wanted to impress his boss. But mostly he wanted to finish the fight quickly, so he could rush to the Assassin's side. He wanted to witness with his very own eyes the strongest moves from his boss.

Using all his strength, Poisson Dagger hit Mender in her left shoulder, creating a cut which began to bleed.

Mender saw the blood and just grinned and yelled, "Let the battle begin." She touched her cheek to her shoulder.

Crazy bitch. Why is she excited when she is bleeding?

Mender returned the attack and managed to cut Poisson Dagger on his right arm.

The bitch cut me! How did she do it? I do not have time to waste. I must finish this and go to my master.

Poisson Dagger called his demon *Eligos* to merge with him. His long dark hair turned blond, and his new sword now looked like a double-blade lance, and stronger than before.

Poisson Dagger swung his most powerful *double-blade evil Tizona* on Mender. When he said the words, both sides of the swords increased its size ten times with a mighty burning fire.

Mender, tried to block the attack, but the fire coming out of the new Tizona was too strong. She managed to block one of the blades, but the fire burnt her skin and the other blade stabbed her badly. She fell on the ground unconscious.

Poisson Dagger thought she was dead, because of his mighty blow, and he left to watch the incredible battle of his master, the Assassin.

~*~

Something had been calling to the hearts of the elders in New Hope Trinity Church. The elders were uncomfortable, but they did not know why.

It was not a service time, it was just a little past midday, but a force stronger than themselves, drove them to go to the church building, where surprisingly Pastor Rick was dedicating some time to prayer.

Pastor Rick normally prayed at home, in his own quiet space, but he felt unsettled and overcome by the need to visit the church and pray there and so he did.

Elders flocked in like ducks in a row and without even stopping to greet each other they entered the church building praising and worshiping the Lord.

When Pastor Rick realized he was in the middle of the group interceding before God and the whole group of elders around him in a prayer chain. They did not know what they were praying for or who they were praying for, the only words that come to their minds was "Precious Team". They did not know if that Precious Team was the elders or someone else, but they could not stop. They knew they had to intercede and pray for the Lord's intervention.

~*~

The Lord of The Night was able to see lightning in the sky coming from the fierce battle of these two mighty warriors in Knockemstiff. *I underestimated my rivals.*

Then the unexpected happened, Warrior

blocked a mighty attack and cut Assassin's left leg, with a curve twist of his sword.

It seemed Assassin saw his own blood for the first time. With a voice of command he called for *Malphas* and merged with his demon.

~*~

At first Warrior did not see any change with the transformation, but he did notice that the speed and the strength in the blows were increasing. He began having trouble keeping up with the battle.

And then, Warrior wasn't able to see Assassin or his position. He had to block the attacks using his senses.

Still, the Assassin's speed was too fast.

Warrior was first bleeding from his right arm, then his right leg, then both arms and legs.

The Assassin was using the invisibility power of his demon to create his most fierce technique the *Deadly Invisible Sword*.

Warrior knew he was losing the battle. *If I do not see him, I cannot cut him. Focus, Warrior, and remember your training."*

Warrior then closed his eyes and started using his spiritual power and senses. Then he started looking at the shadows of his rival.

He was now able to block the attack, although he was still not able to fully see the Assassin, just the movements of his shadow.

After analyzing and trying to predict the blows and getting stabbed many times in the process, Warrior finally managed to predict the next movement and with a mighty swing, he slashed the Assassin.

He didn't know where he had hit, but Warrior could see the blood moving along the Assassin's shadow.

~*~

"Stand up. You must hurry" said the Elite Commander to Mender as she returned to consciousness. "Run to Warrior. He needs you now."

Mender, touched her burnt skin and wounds, using her healing powers and headed to the battle.

She quickly slipped around Poisson Dagger who was so excited with the great power of his master that he did not even see her when she passed him and headed up the mountain.

When she reached Anthony she cried, "*Warrior, Fusion.*"

Immediately the crossed hilted wide curved steel blade Mameluke sword mingled with the light thin blade Espada Ropera Sword creating a final lethal weapon, a very large and thick English *Double Rapier Sword* flashing immeasurable light.

The light prevented Assassin from knowing

whether the swordsmen were coming head-on or from behind.

The sharpness of the light shot over the battle area and obliterated any other objects near them and would blind any other opponents that may be considering joining the conflict.

Warrior swung a mighty attack toward the approaching shadow of the Assassin, and stabbed him, forcing him to stop. The light also blinded Poisson Dagger at the same time.

But the Assassin did not falter. He went for his ultimate killing technique the *Honjo Masamune Dark Tornado.* The speed of the Assassin became a dark tornado with just the lightening of his mighty sword stabbing his opponent and throwing him to the ground.

"The battle is over," he said.

The Assassin didn't appear to notice the second Rapier sword coming from the back until it stabbed him in the chest and he fell on the ground as well.

Then Warrior turned back to his original warrior state and Mender as well, automatically removing the jewels which caused the blindness in Poisson Dagger.

He opened his eyes and saw his mighty master on the ground and his opponent Warrior was now standing in a weak position.

More to his surprise, Mender his former rival

was also standing there.

He swung his sword to kill Mender once and for all, but Warrior blocked him with a move that blew him away.

"Don't worry about him, Warrior. He is mine," Mender said. "Go, finish your own battle."

Once again Assassin stood on his feet and was now back to back with Poisson Dagger, his second in command.

Warrior now faced Assassin and Mender on the other side, faced Poisson Dagger.

"Boss, let us kill these two parasites with one blow," said Poisson Dagger, nodding toward their opponents with his head.

They lunged forward for the final kill.

But Warrior used his super spiritual sense and Mender as well.

"Final Blow," Warrior screamed.

Assassin and Poisson Dagger kept trying to move forward, but instead, they fell to the ground. They had been deadly wounded by the *Mameluke sword* and the *Espada Ropera*.

Darkness overpowered the two evil leaders, and their lives seemed to fade away. They remained unconscious on the ground.

Assassin, Mastema, Poisson Dagger and Ipos were now defeated. And all through the town of Knockemstiff there was light.

Chapter 25

Pastor Good felt the tugging and prompting from the Spirit, but he didn't know what it meant. It was like he was looking through a dark glass.

He dropped to his knees. "Lord God, I feel the call of Your Spirit. Show me what you want me to do."

Fire filled his heart, but God seemed to remain silent. If he could just figure this out he could share with the evangelism team when they met later that morning.

When it was time for the meeting Pastor Good welcomed the group. "I feel the Lord has something special for us to do or to decide today so we need to get started as soon as everyone can take their place.

He glanced around. "Looks like we are all situated. Let us begin by bowing our heads in prayer.

As he opened his mouth to pray the Spirit filled his heart as well as the heart of everyone around him. The whole evangelism team, started interceding in angelic tongues, Praising the Lord.

No one else was around, besides the evangelism team. They had expected to have a meeting but the Spirit had other ideas. Their prayers became a powerful intercession for people they didn't even know.

At a quiet moment, a pause, one of the evangelists stood up. "We must take the day to intercede for "*His Precious Team.*"

Everyone agreed and that day became an intercession day for "*The Precious Team.*" At that moment they thought they were praying for the evangelism team. But something deeper inside Pastor Good made him understand, it was not about them, but about someone else. Who might the *Precious Team* be?

~*~

At Newville town on the east side of Ohio, nothing was new, except the two uninvited guests about to arrive. It was the middle of the day, with a cloudless sky, but somehow as Polyglot and Decipher reached the town, the light from the sun faded.

"It looks like this place is shielded from the outside with the dark and evil power from within," Polyglot said as he and Decipher walked toward their target. The blackest dark presence Polyglot had ever seen emanated from all over the town.

"Look over there." Big Jax gestured toward the

entrance sign of Newville where a dark-skinned muscular guy stood.

"He's leaning against the post with his hands in his pockets, but look at the tendons bulging in his neck," Polyglot said. "He's ready to pounce if you ask me."

~*~

From the time Apollyon had sounded the alert, blood thirsty Black Scorpion eagerly anticipated the great fight to come.

He watched the two uninvited guests approach. An unlikely pair. One was a giant of a man, his arms and neck covered with tattoos of various gangs' symbols. The other was younger and slightly built. Black Scorpion squinted his eyes and tried to recognize them from the descriptions and tales told by his partners.

"Hey, big guy," Black Scorpion hollered. "You look familiar to me. Who are you? And who is your skinny side kick?"

"I am Big Jax and my partner is Josh Pennington."

"Jack-pot!" Black Scorpion slapped his thigh. "So, you are the former boss. The traitor and his new puppet have come to call on us. Nice to have you around here man. I've heard you are a very strong fellow. Surely you will give me a good fight, before you take your last breath."

"And who," Big Jax asked, "are you?"

"Ha! Prepare to tremble when I tell you. I am Nash Sharpe, better known as Black Scorpion and I am the second in command here."

"Only the second in command." Big Jax shook his head and huffed. "That means I need to seek your leader."

Black Scorpion puffed out his chest. "Uh-uh. You first need to pass through me."

"I will be your opponent," the Polyglot said "You do not need to worry about Decipher."

"Got yourself a new name, dude. Cool. I hoped you'd be a worthy rival." Black Scorpion laughed. "No problem to me. I will take the both of you at once." Squinting his eyes again, he studied them, trying to see how powerful they were. But they were really good at concealing their strength level.

"In fairness I have to first give you a chance to surrender," Polyglot said.

Black Scorpion almost fell over laughing.

"All righty then. No more talk." Polyglot turned to Big Jax. "It is time. Decipher, go ahead and find the leader of this town. I will meet you in ten."

He looked at Black Scorpion, then. "Don't worry about Decipher. Your fight is with me and this won't last long."

In the name of the Father, the Son, and the Holy Spirit, Transform, Josh said in his heart.

"Whoa. You must be the blue knight or something," Black Scorpion said when he saw the transformed *Blue - Violet Gemstone Knight* standing before him.

"It is *Polyglot* who you will be fighting, as you are about to find out." Josh stepped forward, and flaming fire dashed from his feet.

"Dude, I like your sandals. That is a good effect. Fire. Hah! I need to get me some fighting shoes like that," Black Scorpion said as he withdrew his Zulfigar sword.

Polyglot pranced back and forth in front of Black Scorpion. "If you were on the Lord's side you would have sandals just like these."

Decipher had turned to go find the town leader so Back Scorpion took this chance to swing on him. But his sword was met in the air. The skinny dude's Messer sword had blocked the attack.

"I told you, I am your opponent," Polyglot said as he swung again with a tremendous strength.

"You're skinny, but it looks like you are stronger than I thought," Black Scorpion acknowledged.

Abdiel the demon and ruler of Black Scorpion appeared behind his puppet holding black chains with razors, axes, and swords at the tip of each chain.

Black Scorpion felt empowered and went for

the second blow, applying more strength this time, trying to hit specific nerve points to neutralize Polyglot.

Polyglot's sword blocked Black Scorpion's hit again. With a sudden twist of his sword the Polyglot was able to injure Black Scorpion.

"Hah. Just a surface cut." Black Scorpion gave him an evil leer. "It is time to get real. *Abdiel*."

Abdiel the demon merged with Black Scorpion's Zulfigar sword, creating a larger and stronger weapon with two parallel sharp blades with a point curve forming a V shape. And, of course, black chains with razors and swords were at the tip of Black Scorpion's new sword. The darkest flame ever seen by humans shot out of the new merged sword.

The *Polyglot* swung his Messer sword which was easily blocked with the new Black Scorpion sword. In between the block, the Zulfigar hit a very special nerve system of Polyglot, thus sending him to the ground.

Black Scorpion could see number ten on Polyglot's right chest, understanding that the Polyglot was not an equal match for him.

"The battle is over," Black Scorpion said in triumph. He swung his lethal sting attack to completely paralyze Polyglot and give him the final blow.

But Decipher blocked the attack with the

strong blow of his Kodachi sword. Black Scorpion flew backwards.

"Are you ok, Polyglot?" Decipher asked.

"I must admit, I thought I could handle him by myself, but a little help would be appreciated."

Decipher laughed.

"Fusion your weapons," the Elite Commander said.

As Black Scorpion looked around to see who had spoken, the double Kodachi mingled with the twenty-four-inch single-edged Messer sword creating a powerful and an incredible Kusarigama.

His eyes widened. His opponents now had a terrifying instrument of elimination.

Two golden sharp blades at the edge of each side of the new weapon pulling with two very large chains with flashes of topaz changed the atmosphere from sunrise to sunset.

"Prepare to go down," Big Jax roared.

The atmosphere was no longer dark, the fusion of the intruders swords brought lightness to this place.

Black Scorpion trembled. But he rallied and flew forward with all his strength to finish these intruders when he saw the Kusarigama sword fly on the air with its golden sharp blades.

"You missed," Black Scorpion said with a

laugh. "My turn."

He saw a blind spot and found an opening to hit and destroy these two with a single blow. With a tremendous surge of victory he yelled, "Zulfigar final sting, kill."

"You think so?" Decipher asked. "This is almost too easy."

He pulled back the two very large chains with flashes of topaz. The weapon flew back to its adversary as a tornado with an indescribable light, flaming like the rainbow's color.

"Cut," Polyglot said.

Black Scorpion tried to turn and block the Kusarigama attack, but it was too late. He saw his evil protector who once was a handsome, muscular being, lying on the ground cut in half and fading away. His Zulfigar sword was broken in two pieces.

Then Black Scorpion's own lights faded away and he knew no more.

~*~

"Lord Jesus Christ, creator of heaven and earth and Lord above all, the battle is yours, let your Holy Spirit guide our heroes and give them the victory," said Ben.

When Deborah and Becky heard that prayer coming out of the small boy, they finally understood how grave the situation was and at the same time, they were amazed on how the

Spirit was using that small boy for intercession.

Jumping and dancing in the Spirit was the task for this day for the two women and small boy, something they could not comprehend, but the Spirit was using them in a very supernatural way.

~*~

The demon Abdiel and its puppet Black Scorpion were defeated.

"One down, and one more to go," Decipher said.

The two warriors continued their walk along the main street following a great darkness that radiated from a not so distant dead-end street.

~*~

When Sammie heard the cry, "Zulfigar final sting, kill," he laughed to himself. "I thought I was going to have to fight, but I did not even have to meet these intruders. Well done, Black Scorpion."

Sammie poured himself a strong drink to celebrate the victory and waited for Black Scorpion when he suddenly felt a strong and lightning presence.

"Too early to celebrate," Decipher said. "Am I interrupting something?"

He knew that voice and when he turned he recognized both faces. "Well, look who's here. Boss and Josh."

"Sammie," said Decipher with a nod.

Millions of thoughts passed through Sammie's mind of the stories he'd heard about Big Jax the Dragon, how strong and fearless he was. "Boss, I could not believe that you turned. But here you stand, and I see it's true. The Dragon has turned into a traitor."

"And I can see you are the leader of this town," Decipher said. "What a shame that I must turn you into ashes. That is, unless you decide to join me."

"In your dreams," said Sammie. "I have always been stronger than you, but you were the Boss." He shrugged and set hid drinking glass down on the nearest flat surface. "I had to respect you and obey your commands. But things have changed. You are a traitor, and I am now the Boss.," Sammie smirked. "I will be highly rewarded for defeating you. *The Lord of the Night* will be pleased."

"Thanks for the information," Decipher said. *The Lord of the Night* is whom I should fight, not you. Step aside and tell me where he is."

Sammie knew his opponent was a very strong dude, so he needed to attack with all his strength from the very beginning and not give a single chance for error or he would be done.

But he could not yet measure or sense the strength level of his opponent. It was as if something blocked his level reading.

He had considered himself the strongest man alive, with his long hair and athlete body. But with his second nowhere to be seen, he needed more help from the very first blow.

"*Botis,* merge," Sammie yelled his demon's name.

Sammie's human shape grew two horns and large teeth filled his mouth. Merged with his demon he presented the form of a gargantuan dragon with impenetrable greenish-brown scales.

His Seven Branched silver Sword was now gleaming with sharp blades on each head. The sight of this warrior was impressive and terrifying.

The strength rank on his left arm displayed the number three, revealing that he was one of the strongest evil rulers to be fought. *Let the traitor try something now.*

"So that's how I used to look," Decipher said. "I guess there is no time to waste." He transformed into The *Blue Musgravite Gemstone Knight* ready for this fight with his double Kodachi swords, and his feet, flaming fire at the same time.

With fire from head to toes, Decipher was covered in lightening and his armor glowed like a billion stars.

Sammie noticed the number three on the

traitor's right chest and nodded. "It looks like we are the same in strength level, let us see who is indeed stronger, evil or light force," the newly transformed Sammie said with his deepened voice. "I always figured light meant lightweight."

Decipher glanced at Polyglot. "Do not intervene, this one is mine."

The metal against metal clanging of the sword fight filled the air. Sammie wanted to end the fight quickly but the traitor blocked every move. He fought harder but they were evenly matched and neither was able to overcome the other.

Dark splashes radiated from each blow of Sammie's strong Seven Branched Sword. Each of the seven blades sought to cut his adversary.

There had to be a way to defeat this dude. Sammie analyzed Big Jax's attacks, slowing down his speed and increasing his strength, hoping to find a blind spot or weak point to strike and go for the kill.

Dark powers hit the surrounding buildings.

Still, Decipher's swings were so strong that something like lightening stars came from his double Kodachi swords with each blow.

Finally, Sammie saw a small opening in Decipher's plan of attack. "I got you now, Boss," he cried triumphantly and went for the kill.

"I'm not your boss any more, I am Decipher,

and I believe it is I who have you."

Both warriors hit each other with one single strike.

Sammie fell on the ground with his left arm bleeding.

Decipher fell on the other side with his right leg bleeding. He scrambled to his feet with a limp.

"It is not over yet." Sammie split his Seven Branched Sword and threw it in all directions with his super speed technique.

Once again Decipher fell to the ground severely injured. One of the seven blades had hit Big Jax on his back.

Sammie roared in victory and leaped forward going for the final blow, but Polyglot blocked it with his Messer sword.

"Polyglot, fuse," Decipher said.

The swords of Sammie's opponents merged into a powerful and incredible Kusarigama.

"That will not change the outcome of this battle," Sammie said."

But somehow the number three on Decipher's chest began blinking and looked brighter, increasing the intensity of the sword.

At the same time, Sammie felt a tremendous increase in power. *Good.* It was time to end this battle. No more time for fun, it was time to kill these two parasites.

He went for his final and master killing swing with the split of his Seven Branched Sword, but this time, not only did the seven branches fly toward his opponents, but the gargantuan dragon fired his killing flames to consume everything in its path.

Sammie threw back his head and gave a victorious dragon cry. Everything was consumed by the gargantuan fire and the seven blades came back dripping blood.

"Battle is over," Sammie said as the smoke faded away.

The intruders lay on the ground, bloody and covered in ashes from the terrible fire.

Decipher raised his head. "Not yet." He threw his incredible Kusarigama blades in the air, aimed toward the dragon's head.

Sammie dodged the blow. "Is that all you got?" He threw back his head again and roared with laughter.

"Cut," Polyglot said as he pulled the two very large chains flashing topaz lights.

"Reduce to ashes," Decipher said

When Sammie realized one of the Kusarigama's blade had sliced the dragon's head and saw it rolling on the ground, he managed to grab the other blade before it cut him.

His hand was reduced to ashes with the topaz flashes of the mighty Kusarigama.

What could have happened? How could I lose to the traitor boss and his puppet?

"The battle is over," were the last words Sammie heard.

Botis the demon and his pupil Sammie were defeated.

~*~

The battle is the Lord's. He has the victory, said one of the elders from New Hope Trinity Church. It is time to cast out all evil spirits, Lord Almighty. Deliver us from evil and its forces. Deliver and give the victory to your *"Precious Team."*

They had no idea what was going on, but the Spirit was using them for something greater than themselves.

~*~

"Wipe out the evil in this town. Cast out all demons," the Elite Commander ordered the heavenly army.

Both hero warriors saw the fleet of heavenly soldiers with their swords in combat position and all the dark forces and demons trying to run away after their leaders had been destroyed.

With a single blow of a lightening flashing sword from the heavenly army, it seemed a type of atomic bomb explosion wiped out the whole town's evil spirits and light radiated throughout Newville Town.

Chapter 26

Wherever lawlessness abounded, strife and hate seemed to thrive. Such was the fate of Blueball, a small town abandoned by most humans and ruled by sinister forces.

As the two heroes headed toward the North-East side of Ohio, Janet suddenly felt an overpowering dark force coming from a street that looked more like a small path than a road. "Stop," she said. "Look back there."

An ancient sign announced 'one mile to Blueball.'

"They sure don't want anyone to find this place," Janet muttered as Michael slowed the car and turned down the path.

Half of a mile from reaching the town they heard a horrible bang and clank coming from the hood of their vehicle.

A quarter of a mile further the car shuddered and stopped.

"What's happening?" Michael groaned. "Anthony specifically chose these Mustangs because they were both fast and new." He got out of the car to check the engine and the battery.

Janet glanced down the road toward their

target town. The gravel path ahead was filled with the darkest aura Janet had ever seen. It was like a black fog all along the road. She still couldn't see the entrance of the town.

Michael opened the hood of the car and blinked his eyes.

Janet moved beside him to see what he was staring at.

The inner workings of the car had a hole the size of a large fist.

"Oops." Janet said. "The rental company is not going to like this."

Michael whipped out his cell phone. "Better call for service now before we head on toward the town."

But before he could punch in a number, a voice came from behind. "Who's going to die first? The pretty woman or the old man?"

A slim blonde woman with a raspy English accent, stood at the entrance to Blueball.

Janet took a step forward. "She is mine."

Repeating the secret prayer in her heart, Janet transformed into a *Golden Red Painite Gemstone Knight*, with *Faith Woman* written on her right arm. Her Red Spartan's sandals flamed fire as she ran toward her adversary, blocking all the swords coming from the sky trying to hit her.

"I guess you are going to be the first," the

blonde woman said. "I see your name is Faith Woman. Your name will not help you today. I am *Iku Zai*, better known as *Flying Swords*." She showed her strength level of six in her left arm.

"I cannot say it is nice to meet you," Faith Woman said. "Because it will be just too short and sweet. Flying Swords, prepare to meet your maker for unless you surrender to Him, your days are over."

"Ha. Ha. Ha! Before you die today, I would love to tell you what my name means." Flying Swords laughed in a gesture of mockery. "Iku means violent and Zai means evil, be honored to die by my hands."

"Nonsense!" Faith Woman swung her Chokuto sword with half her strength and managed to graze Flying Swords left arm.

"*Shrewder* go ahead and find the leader of the town, this one, she is mine," Faith Woman repeated confidently.

Shrewder shook his head as if he was not sure it was the right thing to do. But she insisted, and he continued on his way.

Flying Swords tried to stop Shrewder from leaving, but Faith Woman blocked her attack. "Violent and evil woman, I told you, I am your opponent."

~*~

Flying Swords was not yet using all her

strength, she was testing the strength level of her adversary in order to learn how strong Faith Woman was.

But after seeing a drop of her own blood, she was overpowered by the evil coming out of her cursed Japanese sword "Muramasa," a very fine, sharp and legendary evil sword.

The fight was incredible and she drew energy from crashing her Murasama against the Chokuto swords. Both warriors tried to finish one another off, with no success so far.

But in a surprise move Faith Woman blocked one of Flying Swords' attacks and at the same time, managed to cut a deep wound in Flying Swords left leg.

Just a small cut as far as Flying Swords was concerned. She did not let a little blood stop her. Besides, she was a bloodthirsty warrior and enjoyed seeing the thick red liquid, even if it was her own. She'd gone much too long without using her cursed sword. The battle energized her.

Then, once again, Faith Woman managed to cut Flying Swords. This time on her neck.

Coming within an inch of having her throat sliced, Flying Swords decided she'd had enough of the small stuff. Flying Swords cried her demon's name. "Ipos."

Ipos. The ultimate black cat, with jagged

blade teeth, emerald eyes, and muscled body merged with Flying Swords, transforming her into a stronger warrior. With a cat face, and sharp blades as her teeth, Flying swords roared so loud, she was sure Faith Woman's eardrums felt as if they were about to explode. The very thought made her evil grin appear.

The merging also transformed Flying Swords famous weapon, the Muramasa Sword, into what looked like ten individual swords.

Then the newly transformed Flying Swords gave an evil grin. "It is time to die."

Swinging her ten blades, and giving an overpowering roar, Flying Swords sliced into Faith Woman's left arm, making her bleed incredibly. She was no longer able to hide her strength level of seven and it appeared on her chest for anyone to see.

~*~

What is happening? I can hear voices reaching to heaven. What is it Lord? Faith Woman asked in her heart while in the middle of the battle.

"It is the cry of my servants for all of you, take courage and trust in me. I still have five thousand knees interceding and praying for all of you."

"Use your faith and get to Shrewder, you need to merge your weapons to win," the Elite

Commander talked to her heart, reminding her He was with her all the way.

Flying Swords took one look at the rank displayed on Faith Woman's chest and beamed with confidence. "You are no match for me." She straightened her shoulders "*Korosu.*"

When Faith Woman heard the non-English word, she knew it was nothing good. Even though she did not understand, her instinct of survival kicked in and she ran toward Shrewder. The Lord had said they needed to be together to win this fight…and together they would be, if she could do anything about it.

"Hey! What happened? Are you running from me? So soon? No. No. No. You are not going to take away my fun by running," said Flying Swords.

But Faith Woman did not even look back. Her goal was to reach the Shrewder.

Then she felt another sword stabbing her. She felt the hit on the back of her left shoulder.

~*~

Kimura Ichi, better known as *Evil Sword* a Japanese-American with a long braided beard of grey and white and long straggly hair pulled back into a ponytail reaching to his waist, proudly showed his strength level of two.

Holding his wrapped secret weapon, the Kusanagi, which nobody except its owner had ever seen, Evil Sword waited in the middle of the street for his new rival.

Soon he saw a medium size American approaching with great speed. The man dressed like a *Red Painite Gemstone Knight*, with red armor covering his body resembling the flame of a thousand fires and with his name on the right shoulder *Shrewder*.

Strange name for a warrior. Doesn't sound intimidating at all. Evil Sword smirked.

Crossing from left to right and right to left in a zig-zag pattern while running toward him, the Red Gemstone Warrior displayed his military expertise.

Maybe there is more to this guy than his simple name.

As he got closer the *Red Painite Gemstone Knight* swung his previously concealed weapon, an Aikuchi Katana, with great power, thus forcing Evil Sword to step back.

"Nice try." Without even showing his secret Kusanagi sword, Evil Sword managed to block the attack by controlling the wind.

"You are a very strong dude," Shrewder acknowledged.

"And you are not bad for an old man," Evil Sword answered.

"You are the second in strength level," said Shrewder.

"Yes, I am. Luckily for you, I am a worthy opponent. Plan to meet your doom today. No one has seen my sword and lived to tell about it." Evil Sword puffed out his chest emphasizing his strong power and confidence in the battle. "No time to waste. I need to finish you before Flying Swords finishes with your partner, which I think must be almost over by now. Are you ready, Old Man?"

~*~

Shrewder showing respect to a very strong warrior bowed. "Let us begin."

When Evil Sword released his secret Kunasagi, the Shrewder felt a mighty wind almost blowing him away and with it came a big fire ball aiming to consume him, but Shrewder was able to dodge the attack with little effort and let his adversary see the number two on his right chest.

"Impressive, Old Man, who could have thought that you're almost at the same level as me," Evil Sword said with a smirk.

Shrewder shrugged. "It is my turn now. Are you ready?" And this time he used all his strength with his Aikuchi sword meeting the sharp blade of the Kunasagi.

Both warriors flew through the air and swung their weapons. With the mighty strength with each blow, thunder rolled across the Ohio sky loud enough to be heard by all the other team members.

"Shrewder," Faith Woman cried.

Shrewder was distracted momentarily and he felt a mighty blow on his left arm from Evil Sword. *Bad move.* His arm felt as if it had been dislocated.

"What happened, Old Man? You lowered your guard and lost focus. Come back. Don't worry about your partner. What can she do with only one arm? She is done. Get your mind back on the fight."

But Evil Sword's words were drowned out by the sounds of the saints who were praying.

"I can hear them Lord. I can hear their cry reaching to your throne," said *Shrewder.*

"Yes, my servant, they are thousands praying and interceding for my *Precious Team.*"

~*~

"Fusion," Faith Woman cried.

Michael's hand-forged, tampered Aikuchi Katana merged with her straight single-edged Chokuto. The weapons met in the air creating a unique huge silver Javelin with its tip on fire.

Straight and precise in reaching its target, the javelin resembled a huge silver bird in flight with a glowing, fiery-beak and streams of fire like feathers trailing along the mid-section and end of the blade. A huge golden metal chain with blades on each link, increased the power of both warriors and allowed the bleeding of Faith Woman to thicken and stop.

The hero warriors stood back to back as they had learned in their training and each faced their adversary.

When Flying Swords went for this thousand swords attack she was easily blocked by the new weapon of Shrewder and Faith Woman.

The chain hit Flying Swords' neck and cut her severely. Blood poured down her body.

At this, Evil Sword, released his most powerful attack with his Kunasagi, increasing the ball fire by a thousand and controlling the wings.

Faith Woman and Shrewder were caught in the middle of the fire.

From the evil grins on their faces Flying Swords and Evil Sword obviously thought that the battle was over.

The silver Javelin stabbed Flying Swords through her neck and when pulled back by Faith Woman, the head of Ipos rolled on the ground. Both Flying Swords and Ipos were no longer in battle, game was over for them.

When Evil Sword saw this, he got infuriated and screamed the name "*Legion*" merging himself with the demon. Evil Sword now had a glorious evil crown and longer arms, controlling a tornado-force wind.

Evil Sword then said *"Breath of Satan."* The mightiest wind tornado force ever seen by men rose up from the ground with a big black hole in the middle, swallowing everything in its path.

In the center the tornado Evil Sword stood and aimed his Kunasagi at both opponents.

They were caught up in the black hole and found themselves fighting in the spinning tornado, when out of the walls of the tornado the mighty Kunasagi sword appeared in a speed sound cutting the right arm of Faith woman.

When Shrewder saw this, he managed to kick Faith Woman out from the middle of the tornado and got her outside of the battle.

She was now armless and could do no more to help physically toward the battle. Still she held fast to her faith. She still had her feet.

~*~

Pastor Good and his team thought they saw some sort of vision.

A beautiful team of warriors and angels appeared before them, fighting fiercely the power of evil.

The evangelism team could not understand what they were seeing at that moment, all they could do was to intercede and continue praying.

Maybe sometime they would learn the interpretation.

~*~

Shrewder focused on Evil Sword.

"You are finished," Evil Sword said. "Resign yourself. The battle is over."

Sharp blades swirled inside the wall of the tornado, and a consuming fire narrowed the little space remaining in the center.

Shrewder felt a stabbing pain on his left leg and then the release of blood. He had no choice and went for the ultimate killing technique, one he hoped he would never use. It was so powerful that he himself feared it. "Lightening swords," he screamed.

The long silver Javelin with the linked blade chain began spinning from the center of the tornado to all sides, cutting the tornado walls and breaking through.

Then a much larger Aikuchi double sword with white flaming fire appeared from the sky, hitting Evil Sword and paralyzing his two legs.

The fierce tornado disappeared and the big fire ball fell to the ground as ashes on the ground.

Faith Woman was severely hurt, Shrewder needed to take her out of here and get her to the Emissary.

"Nice touch," Evil Sword said, "But the battle is not over until one of us is dead."

"It is over for now," Shrewder said. "Live for now and die another day." He scooped Faith

Woman into his arms and ran.

When he came upon a slow moving creek he stopped.

"What about the car?"

"Pray for a miracle," Michael said as he carefully laid Faith Woman in the grass.

He dug mud from the bank with his hands, carrying it back to Faith Woman and packed it on the stumps of her arms.

When the bleeding stopped he washed his hands in the creek, and then picked her up again.

"I can walk," she said.

"We are kind of in a hurry here," Shrewder said. "Keep praying. I'm going to try to start the car."

~*~

The Lord of the Night watched the tower of Blueball, from his lofty perch in Hell Town. "At least with *Evil Sword* and *Flying Swords* in this fight, we can be assured this battle is ours."

Moments later, when the sound of the battle was over, the light on Blueball Tower was still off "What did I tell you?" *The Lord of the Night* said. "We won."

With an evil grin he poured himself a drink, lifted a toast to the victory at Blueball, and settled in to watch the remaining battles.

~*~

Back at the Emissary residence, the team began to arrive, *Warrior and Mender, Judge* and *Discerner, then. Decipher* and *Polyglot.*

The *Emissary* was uneasy and eager to talk to the team, and examine their wounds. He knew the battles were not easy and that some of the team members might die or end up with severe injuries, but fortunately, Mender was one of the early returns and was waiting for them.

As each one arrived Mender laid hands on them, and prayed for them, and the Lord healed them.

Shrewder kicked the front door. *Faith Woman* lay unconscious in his arms.

"What happened to her? Where did all the mud come from?"

"With the help of their demons, our enemies were able to penetrate her armor. I had to cover her stumps with mud to keep her from bleeding out on the way home. Can you believe this brave woman wanted to walk to the car?"

Erin placed her hands on Faith Woman and prayed over her. Then she washed off the mud and got Janet into a set of Josh's clean clothing.

The bleeding had stopped completely. The stumps of her arms were covered with flesh. Janet was fully recovered and her wounds were healed. But she was still armless.

~*~

"What do you mean we won? Look over there, you imbecile. Blueball's watch tower light is on. We have not won, we are undone." Apollyon raged and swore. "We lost Blueball. *Evil Sword* and *Flying Swords* have lost the fight."

"At least we still have Slattersville," said *The Lord of the Night.* "And Moonville has not yet fallen. That fight will be the decisive one."

Chapter 27

Standing at the top of the highest building in Slattersville, the former watcher of the town eagerly awaited the arrival of more hero warriors. The Emissary had been instructed to watch and nothing else. "No intervention," came by direct order from the Elite Commander.

After stopping to fix a flat tire, Tadd and Abby were once again on their way.

Discerner recognized the landscape racing past the speeding Mustang.

The *Judge* was an excellent driver and the car approached their target with amazing speed.

Slattersville, strategically located in North-West Ohio was the beginning location for spreading the evil plans of *The Lord of the Night*. And the evil must be stopped.

But this time, there was no invisibility protective shield. This time they were going to Slattersville with one mission in mind, to free the town from evil and bring back the light.

"I haven't told you how thankful I am that our Elite Commander allowed me to be your fighting partner," Tadd said.

His comment thrilled Abby but she needed to concentrate on what was ahead of them. "Who do you think we are up against?"

"I doubt it will be anyone I already know. The prisoners who have been released from Slattersville are the ones most likely sent to rule the newer towns."

"Well, just in case I don't come out of this, I want to tell you—"

"Don't even think it! This battle is the Lord's. He told us not to fear."

"I don't fear, Tadd. Truly I don't. But I am resigned to His will. And I really want to tell you how much I care—"

"Abby. You have to put your feelings aside. You can't be distracted by anything."

She leaned away from him.

"But after this day is over we will rejoice." The Judge stopped the car at a curve half a mile from the entrance of Slattersville.

"Let's stroll into town and see what's up," he said.

As they approached the main road to the town a shirtless man appeared. Not much was visible from this distance except his long black hair.

The man glanced from right to left clearly watching for something or someone.

"Discerner, I expect he is the second-in-command. I'd say the big dog of the town is waiting to see what happens before he gets involved."

When the two warriors were one-hundred feet away the man revealed his strength rank of ten and raised a powerful Viking Ulfbehrt sword. As a threat he aimed his weapon directly at Discerner.

"You must be right," Discerner said. "In the name of the Father, the Son and the Holy Spirit, transform."

The *Purple Diamond gemstone Knight* wielded her Swiss Katzbalger side-arm sword and blocked the enemy's attack without revealing her strength level.

"We have no time to waste, Judge. This one is mine," Discerner said. "Hurry inside and find the leader."

"I can see you've got this." Judge nodded in approval. "I'll leave you to it."

As the man tried to stop Judge from leaving, a flashing-white sword went over his head. He managed to dodge Discerner's attack by a tiny fragment of a second. But he was thrown more than five-hundred feet by the strength of the blow.

"I am impressed," the man said as he rose to his feet. "I misjudged you. Thought you were only gorgeous, but not that strong. Expected a puny weakling. My bad."

He gave her a mocking bow as he walked toward her. "Let me introduce myself. Raff Filtiarn, at your service. I am *Lord of Wolves*. Friends and foes alike call me Wolf."

Without paying the least bit of attention to his words, Discerner raced forward and sent her blow.

Wolf flew over one-thousand feet away this time and scratched his handsome face in the gravel of the road.

"I must take this seriously, or I might lose to this beautiful woman," Wolf muttered. He rose to his knees and then stood. "I wouldn't mind losing to such a gorgeous opponent. What if I surrender right now?" he taunted her.

"It would be in your best interest," she said.

He laughed again and ran toward her. "Time to get real."

She shrugged in distain and ran toward Wolf with her sword swinging.

"*Amaros*," Wolf yelled as a war cry.

Immediately the demon ruler, the cursed one with his two pairs of piercing eyes, one pair in the usual place, and another on the back of his head merged with his barbarian warrior.

The *Wolf*, transformed from a thin Celtic man, into a robust and stronger warrior with a new pair of eyes on his back.

Dark power radiated from his newly upgraded

Ulfbehrt sword, now showing the word *Amaros* on his blade.

"Too bad you are such a weakling you can't fight on your own," Discerner said.

~*~

Reaching his opponent, Judge, displayed number five on his right chest and his warrior name on his right shoulder. As he raised his Dao sword, the blade glowed red and reflected the brilliance of deep aquamarine and emerald. Judge raised his arms and swung his first blow.

Viper, *the Snake* grinned evilly showing his fang-like incisor teeth. Revealing a large number five in his left chest, he counterattacked with his bright and multi-colored Joyeuse sword.

"Not so fast, punk," said the Snake as he blocked the hit. "We're just warming up here."

"You won't get a slow and easy fight with me." Judge swung again and forced the snake to step back.

Snake yelled a French word *"Mastema, fusionnez avec moi."*

"Oh, the little worm is afraid to fight me on his own," Judge taunted. "What a coward."

The demon Mastema merged and Snake transformed into a giant of a creature with two crowned heads. His hair became a thousand poisonous snakes with a black poison liquid dripping from their fangs, melting and consuming everything they bit.

The two-headed crowned giant fairly flew as he slithered forward and was soon close enough to have his snakes bite Judge.

But he blocked and sliced off some of the poisonous hair snakes. As they touched the ground they melted into ashes.

~*~

Wolf licked the blood on his face and threw his demon possessed Ulfbehrt sword toward his opponent.

"You will have to do better than that." For the first time Discerner showed number nine on her right chest.

Wolf's eyes widened at the sight of her stronger rank. "*Amaros, split and cut,*" he yelled.

While still in the air, the Ulfbehrt sword split into two powerful swords.

Not expecting the move, Discerner was only able to dodge one, and she felt a stabbing pain on her back.

She fell to the ground. *I did not see that one coming. How did he do it? Perhaps with the back eyes of his head?* Not even finished with her thoughts, the next blow came within an inch of her neck.

Using one of her karate moves, Discerner responded to the attack with a twist and a mighty blow, which Wolf attempted to block.

But the edge of her *Swiss Katzbalger* blade cut into his right leg.

Wolf noticed the blood and responded with rage. "Time to end this, woman, you are going down."

Discerner did not bother to answer. She stood quietly and watched the final hit to her opponent as if in slow motion. With her spiritual gift, she could find every single particle on the planet. She turned her back on Wolf and threw her mighty Swiss Katzbalger sword.

The sword not only blocked Wolf's attack, but sliced off his left arm. "How did that happen?" *Wolf* asked. "You did not even face me with your attack."

"Allow me to enlighten you before I walk away."

"Walk away? You are so cocky. You think you can beat me?" Wolf said.

"Once again, allow me to clear your mind. Wolf. That is your name, isn't it?"

He stared at her appearing too angry to answer.

"When you stabbed me, I decided to quickly end this worthless fight. You see, there is a great gulf in the power between you and me. I do not like others to know my real strength. My real power is that of a number five warrior. You should feel privileged, not even the other hero warriors know my real strength."

Wolf, the Viking warrior puffed out his chest. "You lie, woman, and it is your undoing."

"Think what you will. I can always see your movements. No matter what you do, I can defeat you without even having to face you."

"*Amaros, kill.*" Wolf yelled.

But soon it was his own head rolling on the ground.

With a single blow from the Discerner the fight was over. Amaros and Wolf were defeated. And she hurried to catch up with Judge for the real battle.

~*~

"We need to end this," Discerner said as she reached the Judge.

"You are bleeding," he said. "Are you ok?"

"Yes, I am. My injury is a small thing.

"Cocky woman." Snake swung his sword toward Discerner.

Discerner easily blocked his attack.

"Well done, Discerner."

"Judge, it is time to end this now," she repeated. "Fusion."

At that moment, the weapons of the heroes merged, creating a double long, cleaver-sharp Bardiche blade. The new weapon could slash through anything. The curved blades flashed amethyst and gold to disorient the enemy as they approached.

The fusion of *Judge* and *Discerner* also duplicated their powers reducing Snakes chances of winning the battle to zero, but Discerner knew he was not aware of this just yet.

The two-headed, crowned giant threw his ultimate killing attack toward both warriors, the incredible Joyeuse sword headed toward his adversaries like a rain of snakes.

But as before, Discerner had the ability to see his movements in slow motion and with this new fusion, she did not need to hide her strength, Judge wouldn't even notice it.

Judge killed all the poisonous snakes with the flames of his new Bardiche blade, burning them to ashes before they touched the ground.

Meanwhile Discerner blocked the slow approaching Joyeuse sword, hitting it so hard that it broke into two pieces and cut off one of the heads of the giant snake.

Discerner shot a glance at Judge. "The battle is over."

"Slide," Judge and Discerner said in unison as they swung their powerful Bardiche swords in the air with a lightening thrust.

One Bardiche sword sliced the snake in two, and the other cut off the remaining head.

The darkness covering the town had finally vanished, Slattersville was free from the power of the demon Mastema and the King Snake.

However, Discerner was still bleeding and the heroes headed to the Emissary residence as they'd been previously instructed.

~*~

From the top of the building the Emissary watched the entire fight for Slattersville. *Incredible, what an incredible power Discerner has.* Then he also headed back to his residence.

~*~

And at Hell town *Apollyon,* and his human counterpart *The Lord of the Night,* observed the towers of their evil towns.

"The watch tower of Newville has been fired on, that is not a good sign. It indicates my warriors have lost the fight."

"How could it be? Who are these warriors and how are they so powerful to have defeated two of my best warriors Sammie and Black Scorpion?" *The Lord of the Night* growled.

"We have lost Newville town now. Let us hope for better results from the other towns."

Suddenly the watch tower of Slattersville lit up as well.

"Oh, no. The King Snake and Wolf have also been defeated."

A messenger from Blueball arrived, gasping for air. "My Lord, our leaders have been defeated."

Another from Knockemstiff gave a full report on each one of the fighting warriors, their strength and skills.

"So they are defeated too?" *The Lord of the Night* was so angry he killed the two messengers for bringing him such bad news.

"Should we move more troops to our Southern town?" asked one of the demons in the room.

"It's too late," *The Lord of the Night* answered. "My strongest leader, with the rank of one was stationed there. No one should have been able to defeat him."

He sucked in a deep breath. "At least, the hero team does not know our secret location. We cannot allow them to discover my presence here and jeopardize my plans."

Chapter 28

Another set of hero warriors arrived at an isolated and apparently abandoned small town, on the West side of Ohio. They noticed visible tunnels at the edge of the town, and evidence of past explosions.

When they approached the entrance of the town they saw a creepy cemetery, and found a sign. "*Welcome to Moonville.*" In small letters, an additional transcription read "*Where death comes to live and life ends in death.*"

"What a creepy message," Psychic said. "Every life eventually ends in death. But this town seems to boast that death comes sooner here. Do you think this is the actual center of all the evil in our state?"

"It doesn't appear that there is anyone around," Marvel said. "But looks can be deceiving."

"Who dares to approach my town? You are either very arrogant or extremely stupid to come here."

Marvel turned and looked toward the cemetery. "Show yourself if you have the guts to face us."

"Are you scared, boy? You should be." A Roman Gladiator appeared out of the dark shadows. The man rising from behind a tomb appeared to be over six foot tall. His head was covered with a metal helmet and bronze face mask with eye slits giving off an evil glint.

"I am the Panther." The gladiator held up his Crocea Mors sword ready to slice and kill. "Welcome to your doom. However, I only fight men and you look like a strong fellow. I shall enjoy the battle."

"Hello there. I'm Marvel, and I take great pleasure to be your opponent today," Chris said.

The gladiator glanced at Psychic. "I do not fight women, unless I must. You can hang around until I finish off your partner, but I suggest you meet my boss, I am sure she would love to fight you."

He nodded in a gesture that she should go ahead and enter the town.

While the gladiator concentrated on Psychic, Marvel prayed the secret prayer in his heart and transformed into a *Jeremevite Gemstone Knight.* He flexed his shoulders sending brilliant flashes of blue and yellow light toward Panther.

"Game on, kid," Panther screamed as he swung the *Crocea Mors,* and cut Marvel's hand.

I shouldn't have been showing off. It's my own fault he caught me off guard.

Panther grinned. "My yellow-death has cut you. Just wait, you will soon start losing your senses."

The gladiator laughed out loud as he lunged for the second strike,

Now that he was paying attention, Marvel effortlessly blocked the attack with his Swiss Sabre.

As they'd been trained, he observed the skill and strength level of his opponent. He held back the use of his full strength until he'd blocked Panther's second blow.

Then Marvel was on the attack and sent Panther to the ground. "I wonder how strong you are, dude. Give me all you've got."

"Thought you'd never ask." Panther thrust and swung until his weapon, *yellow death*, split into ten poisonous daggers.

But Marvel blocked all the daggers. Every single one. "Come on. Is that all you got?"

Panther displayed his strength level number nine on his left chest.

"How sad. I expected a glorious fight," Marvel said as he displayed the number six on his right chest.

"You are too cocky, boy. You ain't seen nothing yet," Panther growled. "*Asmodee,*" he called his demon's name.

The gigantic moth with brilliant eyes, and its

mouth full of sharp pointed teeth, opened dull-brown wings extending them to the horizon and merged with Panther.

The newly transformed Panther now looked like a giant gladiator with the face of a black panther having sharp bladed teeth. The huge wings of the moth radiated a poisonous smell spreading throughout the air.

"You are mine, boy." The giant gladiator threw his ultimate attack with his Crocea Mors, now having hundreds of blades coming out of his teeth and flying over the sky to cover Marvel with the deadly wings of terror.

Marvel was trapped and wrapped into the wings of his rival, while hundreds of blades hit his body.

"Look at all the blood on the ground," Panther yelled a victory cry. "I won."

But Marvel had not given up. The moth had not smothered him, nor had the blades killed him. "Slice," he commanded.

His Swiss Sabre penetrated the wings of the merged Moth and Panther.

The wings fell away and Marvel stood exposed. He was covered in blood and gasping for air.

"Ha! I will soon finish this," Panther called.

"Look at yourself," Marvel said as he backed away a few steps. "Notice where the pool of blood at your feet came from."

Panther glanced down at himself and saw the streams of blood. He gave Marvel a bewildered look. "Did you re-generate yourself?

Marvel shook his head. "You are no match for me."

Panther tried to lift his foot and move forward, but he just fell to the ground while Marvel walked away.

Panther and Asmodee were defeated and light penetrated the cemetery.

~*~

Psychic approached an extremely beautiful woman with short bobbed hair and deep green eyes.

"I am *Pat Williams* better known as *Python.* Who are you and why are you coming to my town?"

"Your town? Not for long," Psychic said. "I am Sandra, but you can call me *Psychic."*

She transformed at that very moment into the *Pink Jeremejevite Gemstone Knight.*

Then Python showed her strength level of four and headed to her opponent with all her strength. The blows hitting so hard, her bloody Yamashita's sword displayed rays of fire coming out of the two swords when they met.

Psychic blocked the attack and responded by hitting as hard as she could. Psychic managed to cut Python's already short hair.

"Didn't think I needed a haircut," Python said. "You must rank high to get that close to me."

Psychic revealed her rank of number four on the right side of her chest.

Python's green eyes widened and she called her demon's name "Samael."

"What a coward." Psychic shook her head as she witnessed the merging.

The Yamashita's sword with the black king snake handle and a Black Python face with sharp poisonous teeth merged with her demon, the new Python became much stronger than a level four warrior.

She proudly swung her new snake sword with all her strength and managed to cut Psychic on her left arm.

Severely injured, with no time to lose, Psychic tried to dodge the second blow.

Python bit Psychic in her back with her poisonous teeth.

"I got you," said Python, and reared back for an even stronger attack. "Prepare yourself for *the python's cut.*

Although Psychic was expecting the head of the snake and tried to dodge it the new snake sword hit her right leg.

Psychic fell to the ground bleeding. The venom was so strong Psychic started to lose consciousness, when she felt another strike on her right leg.

The indescribable pain revived her senses and she noticed she no longer had a right leg.

"Die," cried Python.

In the nick of time Marvel blocked the attack with his Swiss Sabre. "Merge," he said.

His weapon merged with Psychics and created a long, broad flying axe with a two-edged blade on a lengthy pole with a silver chain attached.

The new weapon appeared as a huge constellation in swirling motion and in varying heights, hovering between the heroes and Python.

Then Marvel touched Psychics body, her injuries were healed, and her leg was miraculously restored.

"What kind of magic is this?" Python asked.

"It's no magic at all, just the gift of miracles from the Spirit working through me. But enough talk," Marvel said. "It is time for the evil in this town to die."

He threw the flying ax into the air, but Python managed to dodge the hit.

"You missed," she hissed.

"Slash," Psychic screamed as she pulled the silver chain.

The weapon returned slashing Python on her left leg.

Marvel swung the ax once again, and this time, he pulled the attached chains at the same time. The mighty ax flew past Python in a swirling motion and returned with power like a huge constellation and cut into Python's right arm.

"Evil Cut," Python yelled. Her snake sword flew through the air. Her sharp teeth flew from her mouth and headed toward the heroes.

The pair of warriors dodged all the sharp blades from the teeth as well as the sword.

Psychic saw darkness covering the sky and threw the silver chain to heaven, where the weapon met Python's snake sword.

The snake sword cut the silver chain. Psychic gasped.

But, Marvel had already pulled back on the chain before the snake sword cut it. The momentum of the weapon had already turned. The flying ax crushed Python's head. And the battle was over.

The head of the *Python's demon* was now flat on the ground and the darkness vanished from Moonville.

The whole area was filled with God's glorious light.

~*~

An incredibly loud voice boomed from an unknown location. "*It is not over yet.*"

Lightening flashed and thunder rolled across the sky before all the area of Hell Town faded into the darkness.

Lord of the Night and his master Apollyon were now afraid and began to prepare for their next movement, thankful that the hero warriors still did not know about their location.

After his unbelievable defeat at Blueball, Evil Sword retreated to the main headquarter to meet with his fearless leader, *The Lord of the Night.* He needed healing and had to give account for his failure.

He only hoped he would live through the coming inquisition.

Chapter 29

After the victorious but wounded warriors had all returned to the Emissary residence, Erin laid hands on each one of them for healing.

The next morning Janet was not reconciled to remaining armless. "I am Faith Woman. And I am praying for my hands and arms to be restored. I have faith for a miracle."

Then Marvel reached out his hand and her two arms grew out once again. Faith Woman clasped Chris's hands. "Since God patched up the hole in our Mustang, I knew He would give me back my fighting arms." Her voice was full of happiness.

"Tell us what happened to your car," Chris said.

By turns, Janet and Michael told of their experience at Blueball.

When they finished, Chris glanced at Erin.

"I think it is time for Marvel and Mender to team up and heal the five Mustangs. As God's ambassadors, we need to return them to the car rental in better shape than we received them."

Erin grinned. "Okay everyone. Let's do this right. Come on outside and lift up your voices in praise to the Father while Marvel and I lay hands on the rentals."

After the blessing on the cars the team returned to the great room and shared their stories of battle and what they had learned from them.

With each story Michael either praised or gave advice on battle techniques.

"It's obvious we still have unfinished business," Big Jax said. "They will just take Kimura Ichi to the witch doctor and try to put Blueball back into business."

"You are correct." Anthony nodded his agreement. "This battle is not over yet. Our Elite Commander revealed that the person in command is no other than *The Lord of the Night.* He is the head of all the evil operations in Ohio, but even his underlings have never seen him."

"Of course, our Elite Commander knows the real name of The Lord of the Night," the Emissary said. "While we wait for His direction let us pray, study, and worship."

Anthony held out his hands. "Let's have a group prayer right now."

One by one each of the team members cried out to God in praise and thanksgiving and dedicated their allegiance for anything that was yet ahead of them. The Emissary finished with a blessing for the heroes.

"You can now return to your respective families and jobs. Don't forget to practice your training and go over what we learned in the battle yesterday. We will meet back here at my home one month from now."

Josh punched Big Jax on his bulging bicep. "Hey, big guy. Guess it is time for you and me to find honest jobs."

Big Jax frowned. "Don't you remember the deal when we moved here?"

"What are you talking about?"

"Daniel said until we have our state cleaned up he would give us room and board in exchange for helping him maintain this place."

"Right." Josh shrugged. "But we can't keep imposing on him."

"I'm sorry," Daniel glanced at his two guests with sorrowful eyes. "I should have offered to pay you something as well."

"That's not—" Josh was mortified that Daniel thought he was asking for more.

~*~

That evening, at New Hope Trinity Church, Janet played the organ as she had never played before. Her God-restored hands flew across the keys with spirit-filled power. The healing music penetrated the sanctuary.

Reverend Robert Milton stared at her with

what could only be called an awestruck daze. The corners of his mouth lifted in a contented smile.

However the darkness and demon influence was still apparent.

The muscles of the other heroes automatically stiffened. They were preparing for action as soon as they got word from the Lord. Surely after cleaning up the five evil towns they could expect peace to reign in their church home.

"Stand firm. It is time to confront Reverend Milton and Beth Cooper. It is time to release my people from the influence of *Succumbus* and *Perdix*. The Discerner is in charge of this battle," the Elite Commander spoke to each of their hearts.

When the service was over and the members of the congregation visited among themselves, the team had an impromptu meeting.

"Judge, please tell Reverend Milton we need to speak to him after every one else has gone," Discerner said.

Marvel twisted his head from side to side as he searched the sanctuary. "Where is Beth?"

Discerner glanced around. "She has already left the building."

"I'll go find her." Marvel fast walked out of the sanctuary.

Then Discerner held out her hands to the others. "Let's hold hands and give a quick silent prayer while the other members of our congregation take their time in fellowship before they leave the sanctuary."

When the heroes finished and raised their heads Reverend Milton stood beside them.

"I'm here," he said, looking only at Janet. "I can't remember your organ rendition being more beautiful or more powerful."

"Thank you, sir. But we have something more serious to discuss with you." Faith Woman nodded to Discerner.

"Okay, Abby, how can I help you?"

"Robert Milton we know about your affair and lascivious behavior."

Reverend Milton's face filled with anger. "How do you dare accuse me?"

"We dare, because you have betrayed the trust the Lord placed on you by allowing you to be our reverend."

Robert's eyes widened.

"Plus, you have damaged the reputation of Christ's church. You have hurt the entire body of Christ."

"I'm back," Marvel said. He had a tight grip on Beth who seemed ready to bolt at any moment.

She was surrounded with darkness and when she reached Reverend Milton the mighty demoniac presence overpowered Robert, and he fell to the floor in a dead faint.

The demon presented as a four headed wolf and lunged toward Discerner.

"In the name of the Father, the Son and the Holy Spirit, transform."

Her Swiss Katzbalger sword hit the four headed wolf, slicing off one at the neck. The head immediately fell to the floor and disintegrated.

"You will not win." The demon adopted its spinning tornado form. The church pews rose into the air and flew through the stained glass windows. The teeth from one of the remaining three heads knocked into Discerner.

Then a small elflike creature jumped on Discerner and began to wrap her in evil black chains.

However Marvel had her back and sliced off the elf creature's head with his Swiss Sabre sword. Flames rose up to consume Perdix, and the little demon was banned from New Hope Trinity Church.

Freed from the smaller demon, Discerner swung another blow at Succumbus and sliced the wolf creature into pieces.

The image of the chopped pieces of the wolf creature faded away like dust.

Robert revived and sat up. He glanced at the

ruined sanctuary. "What happened?"

"This is the result of sin," Discerner said.

As if in a movie, the Elite Commander allowed a replay view of the battle. Both Robert and Beth saw the heroes in their glorious armor.

"That—those ugly creatures were controlling me?"

Discerner nodded. "I take it this is not the side they showed to you."

By now the heroes had returned to their normal appearance.

Robert relaxed. "Are they really gone now?"

"Now is the operative word." Abby sat on the floor beside Robert and took his hand. "Luke 11 says 'When the unclean spirit is gone out of a man, he walksthrough dry places, seeking rest; and finding none, he says I will return unto my house whence I came out. And when he comes, he finds it swept and garnished. Then he goes he, and brings with him seven other spirits more wicked than himself; and they enter in, and dwell there: and the last state of that man is worse than the first.'"

Robert's face drained of color. "Then what am I to do?"

"Luke doesn't leave us there. Later in the chapter we learn more. Verse 28 says, 'Blessed are they that hear the word of God, and keep it.' You see, it's when the demon returns and finds an empty house, he knows he can return. We must keep our hearts and minds filled with God."

"I want that."

"Jesus fills us with light. And the demons cannot abide light."

"I used to walk with God. Do you think he can ever forgive me?"

"Of course. He has been waiting for such a moment as this." Abby motioned for the others to come close and lay their hands on Robert.

"I thought it was a dream, but it was real, wasn't it. All those things I've suffered were real." Tears ran down Beth Cooper's face. "Can you pray for me too? I want Robert and me to do the right thing. I've wanted him to marry me for a long time."

Robert clumsily rose to his feet. "Beth, I am so sorry that I used you so callously."

Hope filled her face.

"When I realized what I felt for you was not love I was afraid to break it off."

"What are you saying? How can you say that after assuring me over and over that you loved me?"

"But Beth, you can't really think we were in love. Not when you invited Nina to join us that night. That's when I knew for sure." Robert reached his hands toward her. "But I am sorry for the hurt I have caused you. So very sorry."

"You. You bastard!" Beth slapped Robert so hard red marks remained as she ran from the sanctuary.

"So you see," said the Elite Commander audibly so that even Robert could hear. "Our work is far from over. In this church my redemption work has just begun."

~*~

At first, Janet didn't recognize the phone number that appeared on her cellphone. "Hey, that's New York's area code."

She clicked accept and placed the phone to her ear. "Janet speaking."

"Hello Janet, nice to finally reach you, Pastor Good on the line."

"It's great to hear your voice Pastor Good. I've missed you and our church family in New York."

"And we have missed you. In fact, that is why I'm calling."

"I am sorry. How rude of me. How may I help you, Dear Pastor?"

"That's the dilemma I'm in. Because I honestly do not have the slightest idea."

"Intriguing. Shall we brainstorm then?"

"I've missed our brainstorming sessions. But anyway here is the situation. I have been instructed by the Lord to take our evangelism team, the full twenty members, and head to your location."

"Really? How cool is that."

"In fact, we're on the way as we speak."

"I can't wait to let the others know about this." Janet bounced like a kid in her excitement.

"Sorry I didn't reach you earlier. It wasn't for lack of trying."

"Yeah. Sorry about that. We've been rather busy. I don't think anyone on the team has been available for a while. But this is great news. Truly."

"The thing is. I couldn't wait until you answered. I was told to drive to Ohio, and I am leading two other vans."

"Great. I can't wait to see you."

"That's good. Because we will reach Clanston in less than twenty minutes."

"Yay!" Janet screamed out her young nephew's favorite exclamation.

"Now you're making me think of Ben." Pastor Good chuckled.

When she calmed down, Janet gave specific directions on how to get to Michael's Reeves residence. "Most of us are here for a, well, sort of a victory celebration."

Janet hung up and swiveled to face the others.

"Listen up, guys. You probably gathered that was Pastor Good on the phone. But what you don't know is the whole evangelism team is on their way from New York, and will be here in about twenty minutes. I am so excited."

"That is an understatement," Abby said.

"I was expecting something like this," Anthony said. "The Elite Commander spoke to me last night about a very special team coming to work with us. But I sure was not expecting it to be our friends from New York."

"Did He tell you what his plans are for the evangelism team?" Janet asked.

"You realize they are not warriors like us." Anthony let his eyes roam around the group. "But the Lord certainly has an important task for them. The towns have been free now from the power of the evil, even the evil rulers have been set free, they are not yet aware of it, but they must hear the Word to fill their heart with light or I fear for the worst. Now we must summon the Emissary and the other team members.

"Amen," Abby said. "I will make the calls."

Janet headed for the kitchen to find Deborah.

Always happy to serve more guests, Deborah was already at work preparing a very quick and easy feast. "You know they will be hungry after that long trip."

"After ten hours of driving you can bank on that. And, of course, the rest of us are hungry too," Janet said. "Give me a job. I am sure Abby will join us as soon as she gets off the phone."

Twenty-five minutes later, the New York group arrived at Michael's location. Thirty-five minutes later, Daniel Samuels, Josh, and Big Jax joined the reunion.

Introductions and general information was shared among all of them. And then an impromptu meeting began.

The hero warriors gave information on their tasks and the recent battles with the evil forces, not giving full details, of course, but more of a general outline of what happened.

When they finished, the Emissary stood. "Praise the Lord these five towns are free from evil forces."

Pastor Good smiled and nodded, "I now recognize why we have been sent here."

"Before starting the battles the Elite Commander said He had special plans for these towns. Now that these evangelists have arrived from New York, things are falling into place. The Lord wants you to preach the Good News of Jesus Christ in the five towns.

"Yeah," Abby said. "The towns need to be filled with light, or the darkness will come back and claim them again."

"I was instructed by the Holy Spirit that there were six specific towns to cover and eventually the whole state of Ohio," Pastor Good said.

The hero warriors looked at each other. Then

Anthony opened his mouth to speak. "As for now we only know about five towns. We are waiting to hear more from the Lord."

"How long are you going to be here?" Becky asked. "Have you arranged for a place to stay?"

"To tell the truth, we were in a hurry to get on the road," Pastor Good said. "I know we should have planned ahead, but we haven't made any arrangements so far."

He winked at Janet. "Of course I tried to call."

"I am so sorry I wasn't available," Janet said.

"No problem. But it would be nice if you guys can show us a hotel nearby where we can settle for our first week, while we discover more about the towns and places where we will preach the Good News."

Deborah nodded to Michael and he winked at her.

"We have several rooms here where some of the evangelists can stay. It might be a bit crowded but, it would be our honor to host you here."

"I also have space for the remaining brothers at my residence in Slattersville," Daniel said. "That is one of the towns where you will be preaching."

"Praise the Lord." Pastor Good grinned from ear to ear. "Isn't it marvelous how He provides all our needs?"

The evangelism team divided into five groups of four accompanied by two warriors in each group. The very same ones that had defeated the evil forces at each town.

"I will keep in contact with all the groups and guide them," Pastor Good said.

Now that everyone knew their mission, the meeting finished with praise and worship.

Fourteen of the evangelists went to the Emissary's location and the remaining seven, including Pastor Good stayed at Michael's location.

Chapter 30

A month had passed and *The Lord of the Night* angrily threw black paint on the remaining windows of the buildings of Hell Town.

Not only had he lost the five towns, but the busybodies from New York had taken them over.

The Lord of the Night had tried to recruit new followers, but he could not even get near these towns.

From dawn to dark the usurpers had repaired, and cleaned the old buildings. Finally splashing them with colorful paint.

Now the towns were disgustingly light, bright, and welcoming. Preaching and the singing of hymns greeted the returning families.

He gnashed his teeth. His former towns were now protected by the forces of light. Darkness was repelled from them.

The demon forces could not abide the light. Something needed to be done about it.

~*~

In the middle of the night, words came to each of the hero warriors. "Prepare for the worst battle ever. Everyone on the team must go."

The Emissary woke from a deep sleep. "You

will face your worst enemy, get ready to fight with the team," said the Elite Commander.

Phone calls raced across the wireless terminals from one team member to another. They were all awake and alert knowing a fierce battle was coming, yet they did not know when or where.

Each hoped someone else on the team had more information.

With one call from the Emissary, a meeting was scheduled for the following morning at the mansion.

~*~

It was 9:00 o'clock on a beautiful spring morning in May, when nineteen people from Clanston descended upon the Emissary's mansion.

Pastor Good and the other six New York evangelists staying at Michael's, as well as Deborah, Becky, Ben, and Robert Milton along with the hero warriors had piled into three vehicles.

"Welcome to my humble abode." The Emissary met them on the front porch.

"I'd hoped we could get here earlier," Pastor Good said as he stepped onto the front porch. "I wanted to go over some things with the evangelist teams before they head out this morning."

"Do you mind suspending the preaching today and asking your worship teams to stay here?"

"If that would help you. We will do anything you need for us to do."

"Wonderful," the Emissary said. "We need your prayers today more than anything."

"It is an honor to be part of this heavenly work. Go and do what you have been entrusted to do. We will stay and form a prayer chain for you, not only here with the small group of believers in our newly restored towns, but we will also call all the members in New York."

Reverend Robert's eyes lit up in appreciation. "Praise the Lord. That is an outstanding idea. The warrior families can call the faithful from Clanston as well."

As the Emissary had requested, those who were not hero warriors, except for Pastor Good, went inside the mansion while the hero warriors held their meeting outside.

Pastor Good finally understood whom he and his team was praying for a month ago and who that "Precious Team" was.

Each of the prayer team called families, friends, and any pastors they had contact with, and requested a special time of prayer throughout this day.

Their contacts called others and by the time

the warriors left, thousands of people were kneeling in prayer. Such is the faithfulness of believers that they were willing to pray for this team that was unknown to most of them.

~*~

Before they left for battle, a meeting began at the training place, outside.

All of the Warriors transformed into shimmering Gemstone Heroes.

Black *Garnet Gemstone Knight,* displayed Warrior on his right arm. His matching team member displayed her name of Mender.

Anthony grasped Erin's hand and held it up. "Hero warrior set number one is ready."

Blue Musgravite Gemstone Knights displayed Decipher, and Polyglot.

"Hero warrior set number two is ready." Big Jax's voice boomed out.

Red Painite Gemstone Knights displayed their names of Shrewder, and Faith-woman.

Michael tipped his head. "Hero warrior set number three is ready."

Red Beryl Gemstone Knights displayed the names Judge and Discerner.

Following Anthony's lead, Tadd held up Abby's hand. "Hero warrior set number four is ready."

Pink Jeremejevite Gemstone Knights displayed their names of Psychic, and Marvel.

"Hero warrior set number five is ready," said Sandra.

The *Emissary* also appeared in his full armor. "The Elite Commander has called me into battle this day as well."

Pastor Good raised his hand. "Praise the Lord for giving me the opportunity to see His mighty power through his servants."

Then the Elite Commander spoke to the team in a loud voice "Hell Town is your destination. You will find the ultimate evil leader there. Prepare for battle. This is not going to be easy, but I will be with you every step of the way."

"*The Lord of the Night* is in Hell Town," Decipher said.

Anthony looked at Big Jax. "Where is Hell Town located?"

"I heard rumors about it a long time ago. According to the stories, Hell Town is in a hidden location, right in the center of Ohio," Daniel said.

"Yes." The Elite Commander spoke audibly. "This is the ultimate location for controlling all operations and the other five towns. "Since it is not visible to human eyes, I will guide you there."

Chapter 31

The white cloud guided the Emissary, who in turn led the hero warriors right into the center of pure evil where Apollyon reigned along with *The Lord of the Night.*

It was just a bit before midday when the team reached Hell Town. But with the darkness covering the town it appeared to be midnight.

The eleven warriors transformed for battle.

A masked man clothed in black leather and boots of steel, waited impatiently before a throne at the entrance of Hell Town. He raised his powerful arms and six-pairs of leathery wings overlapped to spread over his head and down to his feet. His golden tan was the perfect background for the smile that revealed exquisite white teeth.

The black face mask was the tell that revealed *The Lord of the Night* had merged with *Apollyon* himself, and was still protecting his human identity.

His second in command stood beside him. Kimura Ichi, a number two ranking warrior, better known as Evil Sword.

With his pitch perfect evil voice, *The Lord of*

the Night said, "Welcome to your annihilation, scumbags."

He turned to Evil Sword. "Let's be done with this foolishness. Wipe them out. Every last one of them."

"This one is mine." Shrewder ran toward his old rival Evil sword. "We have unfinished business."

With a single blow of Evil Swords weapon, Shrewder was thrown to the ground. "Stupid fool. You are no longer a match for me. None of you are."

"Strange," Warrior said. "You sure don't look very strong."

"Hah." Evil Sword spat on the ground. "I will fight you all at once."

"Go," the Emissary said, giving the nod to the hero warriors.

"Not you, Emissary." *The Lord of the Night* raised his fist. "You are mine."

Two battles began. The ten hero warriors faced Evil Sword and raised their weapons.

Then the Emissary transformed from his normal warrior form to his ultimate *Blue and Pink Poudretteite Gemstone Knight.* For the first time he displayed his strength level zero on his right chest.

Holding his Silver Knights of Heaven Sword named *Heavenly Rain,* the Emissary marched toward *The Lord of the Night*, the unknown evil leader behind the mask.

"Way to go Emissary," the hero warriors cried at unison.

"Do not be distracted," the Emissary said without turning his head.

He knew, this was no game. He had no time to measure his enemy's strength, no time for analyzing. He needed to use all his power from the very beginning.

Raising his mighty sword, he said "*Heavenly Rain.*"

Thousands of swords fell from heaven like lightning and blinded anyone in their path. They charged like a super speed torpedo, aiming to slash and slice his adversary.

The Lord of the Night blocked the mighty attack by simply opening his powerful arms and the six-pairs of leathery wings became a heavy metal shield protecting him without even lifting his mighty no-name sword.

His rank number zero on his left chest was visible to the Emissary even though he had been thrown back twenty feet.

"I know all your movements, you will need to do better than that to get closer to me," *The Lord of the Night* said.

This doesn't make sense. We have the same level of strength. Why was I not able to even nick him with my Heavenly Rain sword? He has no wounds at all.

Then the Emissary swung for the second time, adding a more personal touch this time. A special move he'd not taught to anybody, because of its powerful strength. Once again he said "*Heavenly Rain.*"

"You fool," *The Lord of the Night* said. I told you I know all your movements. Show me something new."

Again he opened his powerful arms and six-pairs of leathery wings, blocked all the swords coming down from heaven.

At first he overlooked the swords emerging from the ground. Although he twisted to dodge the attack, one of the swords caught him on his face and the black mask vanished.

~*~

Meanwhile Evil Sword had managed to hurt most of the hero warriors before they fused into their ultimate and most powerful techniques needed to defeat this mighty enemy.

Alone, none of them were a match for this evil demon filled warrior.

A huge silver Javelin flew toward Evil Sword and was blocked and broken into pieces by the mighty warrior.

"*Full Attack,*" Warrior said.

The   remaining   fused   weapons,   the

Kusarigama, Clever sharp Bardiche, Flying Ax, and double English Rapier sword combined into one single lethal attack.

Evil sword tried to dodge all the mighty weapons, but the Rapier Sword stabbed him, and the chains from the Kusarigama and Flying Ax got him by the neck, while the mighty double long Bardiche swords, cut him into pieces.

As one the team screamed, "*Slice to ashes.*" The hero warriors pulled the mighty chains. Their weapons reversed and beheaded Evil sword's demon. He faded away like the wind and an unconscious injured man laid on the ground.

~*~

When the mask fell away from *The Lord of the Night,* the Emissary could not believe his eyes. The face behind the mask was familiar to him.

How could it be? But he couldn't deny it. His beloved old master *Watsuki Gensai*, stood before him. His *Sensei.*

Without sentiment or a single word, his former instructor rushed him and released his no-name sword with a mighty power. The blow cut the Emissary in several places and threw him backwards.

Finished with their own fight, the hero warriors joined the attack on *The Lord of the Night.*

Even without his mask none of them knew who he really was. They threw all five fused weapons with all their might.

"Split," *The Lord of the Night* said, and his mighty no-name evil sword stabbed each one of the hero warriors at once.

Severely hurt, they dropped to the ground.

The Lord of the Night floated in the air and laughed wickedly.

"He is my *Sensei, Watsuki Gensai".* The Emissary said. "I owe everything I know to this man. I could never defeat him. He is too powerful for me."

"You are right," Warrior said. "You alone cannot defeat him. We must work together as one. Let us fusion our swords and powers to defeat the evil commander."

"I am proud of you Daniel, my worthy student. You have grown a lot since the last time I saw you," Watsuki Gensai, said.

"I see you have also used your knowledge and passed it to others. As a Sensei I am proud. You were always my favorite and best apprentice. I tried to convince you to join me. I tried to bring you to be my right hand, but you are so stubborn with your Godly principles and teaching. What has your God done for you? Where is He now? Where was He when I took your family away? Where was He when I stripped away everything you held dear?"

"He was always there," the Emissary said. "Waiting for me to wake up from my foolishness. Just as He waits for you."

"Bah. You know that is not true. I infiltrated the ranks to be able to train you. And yet, you are still here fighting for your God with this pathetic group of so called Christians. Come *Deshi.* Join me and let us rule together. That's what I have always wanted. You will have power, glory, and richness, everything your heart could desire. Come and join me."

~*~

Prayers from throughout the country reached to heaven and even the hero warriors could hear the clamors, the pleading for them in their spirits. The saints did not know why they were praying so hard, but they could not stop.

~*~

"Do you hear them praying for you? Do you honestly think their fruitless prayers will make the difference? Come and join me."

The hero warriors stood on their feet and spiritually connected to one another in their hearts. With this new telepathic connection they could hear each other's thoughts.

Emissary, they all reached out in unison. *You have been chosen by God. We are all here because of you. Our bad experiences and loss have become fruitful for the kingdom of heaven. We cannot turn back now. Fuse with us. Let us end this battle.*

The Emissary squared his shoulders and faced *The Lord of the Night.* "You have betrayed your beliefs. You have turned your back upon the Lord Almighty and today is your day to give accountability."

"Fusion," eleven voices rang out, and the unexpected happened.

The English Rapier sword, huge silver Javelin, kusarigama, sharp Bardiche blade, broad flying axe merged with the "*Heavenly Rain*" creating the ultimate lethal weapon. Each hero held a double Three-Ball battle-worthy mace of ebony stone and facets of diamonds combined with the elegance of rubies and glowed with a piercing silver light.

And all their armor became as white as the snow, flashing like the sun. Eleven warriors now had a new team name engraved on their chest above their rank number *Precious Team.* Directly underneath the new team name was the number zero.

The Lord of the Night was now facing eleven hero warriors with the same strength as himself. However their joining made his opponents one-hundred and ten times more powerful than the demon possessed *Sensei.*

"Is this a joke?" *The Lord of the Night* wasn't really asking a question. "I am merged with Apollyon and no insect will ever win over me. It doesn't matter who you are or how strong you are. You are nothing."

The Elite Commander lifted the veil and showed His Precious Team the heavenly Army, prepared to fight alongside of them. The mighty *Archangel Gabriel* was commander of the heavenly forces.

"Now you are fighting dirty," Apollyon's voice took over the merged body of himself and *The Lord of the Night.* "You brought this on yourselves," he yelled. "*Demons, join.*"

Legions of fallen angels appeared and prepared to fight with Apollyon. *The Lord of the Night* with his countless evil forces gnashed their teeth with impatience, ready to do battle.

Facing them was God's *Precious Team* holding their new fully merged mighty Three-Ball Mace weapons.

Archangel Gabriel gave the war cry as commander of the combined heavenly and human army.

Apollyon and the evil army rushed forward with power and fury.

The muscles of every one of the Precious Team tensed.

"Stand. Stand. Stand firm. Hold. Hold. Hold,"

Archangel Gabriel said. "Let our foes come closer before you respond."

When Apollyon was about twenty feet away, Archangel Gabriel cried "*Engage weapons now.*"

Lightening swords flew on the air and clashed with the evil swords, slicing the demons and reducing them to ashes. Heavenly Rain of eleven pairs of three-Ball Maces, were actually thirty-three metallic balls with sharp point tips which hit the adversaries repeatedly and took them down.

It seemed a grand finale, when an explosion emerged from within the heavenly army and precious team.

Lightning and thunder, and a very concentrated mass of energy emerged from within the center of them and radiated to the outside. The mass of energy reduced everything in its path to ashes.

Hell Town and its leaders *The Lord of the Night, and Apollyon* along with all his evil forces were defeated.

~*~

In the following days Pastor Good appointed leaders to raise a church for each town.

And each town could count on the help of the precious team, now working within these communities, performing healing, miracles, and using their gifts for the sake of the Lord.

Light had triumphed and the heavenly choir sang praises with the assurance that the gates of Hades shall not prevail against the Church.

The team was not yet aware of the big difference and the outcomes of the battles for the evil leaders. Not even The Emissary. They thought that evil leaders could die in the battles and process, but they had not been instructed on the real repercussions of the battles.

Evil leaders and commanders were possessed and fusion with their evil rulers, thus in the battle, only the demons were sliced and hurt. Of course, evil human leaders were severely hurt whenever they fought in their human forms, but when merging with the demons, only demons suffered the hurt and lost. Only an unconscious individual with severe injuries were left at the end of each battles, but the Precious Team did not know it.

Someone needed to tell them and instruct them, but who might that be?

This was the longest day in the life of the heroes, they all had one thing in their minds and it was to set free the towns from evil forces. They did not had the time to think about the human evil commanders, less could they still comprehend, their own strength and how the

Spirit in them made everything possible, they did not yet understand who *The Hero Within* was. But they would learn.

Other Books By the Author:

The Hero Within Series

Language Books

Dr. Yeral E. Ogando comes from a very humble origin and continues to be a humble servant of our Lord Almighty; understanding that we are nothing but vessels and the Lord who called us, also sends us to do His work, not our work. *Luke 17:10* **"So likewise ye, when ye shall have done all those things which are commanded you, say, We are unprofitable servants: we have done that which was our duty to do."**

Mr. Ogando was born in the Caribbean, Dominican Republic. He is the beloved father of two beautiful girls Yeiris & Tiffany.

Jesus brought him to His feet at the age of 16-17. Since then, he has served as Co-pastor, pastor, Bible

School teacher, youth counselor, and church planter. He is currently serving as the Secretary for the Dominican Reformed Church as well as the liaison for Haiti and USA.

Fluent in several languages Mr. Ogando is the Creator and owner of an Online Translation Ministry operating since 2007; with Native Christian translators in more than 25 countries.

(www.christian-translation.com),

The most exciting thing about his Translation Ministry is that thousands of people are receiving the Word of God in their native language on a daily basis and hundreds of ministries are able to reach the world through the work of Christian-Translation.com along with his translation network of 17 websites in different languages related to Christian Translation.

Reviews:
Reviews can be tough to come by these days, and you, the reader, have the power to make or break a book. If you have the time, share your review or comments with me.

Thank you so much for reading *POWER The Hero Within Volume Two* and for spending time with me. You can check out my other books and future books on my amazon page:

https://www.amazon.com/author/yeralogando